Georgia Hill writes romcom published by One More Ch[...] of HarperCollins.

She divides her time between the beautiful counties of Herefordshire and Devon and lives with her two beloved spaniels, a husband (also beloved) and a ghost called Zoe. She loves Jane Austen, eats far too much Belgian chocolate and has a passion for *Strictly Come Dancing*.

www.georgiahill.co.uk

 twitter.com/georgiawrites
facebook.com/georgiahillauthor

Also by Georgia Hill

The Little Book Café Series

The Little Book Café: Tash's Story

The Little Book Café: Emma's Story

The Little Book Café: Amy's Story

(Also available together in a bind-up edition)

The Millie Vanilla's Cupcake Café Series

Spring Beginnings

Summer Loves

Christmas Weddings

(Also available together in a bind-up edition)

The Say it with Sequins Series

The Rumba

The Waltz

The Charleston

(Also available together in a bind-up edition)

Standalones

While I Was Waiting

THE GREAT SUMMER STREET PARTY PART 3

Blue Skies and Blackberry Pies

GEORGIA HILL

One More Chapter
a division of HarperCollins*Publishers*
1 London Bridge Street
London SE1 9GF
www.harpercollins.co.uk
HarperCollins*Publishers*
1st Floor, Watermarque Building, Ringsend Road
Dublin 4, Ireland

This paperback edition 2022

1

First published in Great Britain in ebook format
by HarperCollins*Publishers* 2022
Copyright © Georgia Hill 2022
Georgia Hill asserts the moral right to be identified
as the author of this work
A catalogue record of this book is available from the British Library
ISBN: 978-0-00-858651-5

Printed and bound in the UK using 100% Renewable Electricity
by CPI Group (UK) Ltd

For the ADCs. Thank you for the 'Zoom handholding.'

The Berecombe News

OUR FABULOUS YEAR OF COMMEMORATION CONTINUES!

By: Keeley Sharma

As well as mists and mellow fruitfulness, this autumn also brings our very own film festival, co-ordinated by Patron of the Regent Theatre, Michael Love. Mike is born-and-bred Berecombe and is now a theatre director of international repute. He promises there will be a film to tempt everyone's tastes. Speaking of tastes, Nico, from the Icicle Works, is concocting a special flavour of ice-cream for the intervals. Let's hope it's not World War Two themed or we might end up with frozen carrot and potato in our cone!

The year culminates in the opening of Berecombe Museum's Living Memories Exhibition. Museum director Noah Lydden assures me it will be fascinating to anyone with an interest in the history of our wonderful town. There's a party on the first night, attendance strictly by invitation, which is bound to be a great night, as we all know how much

Berecombe likes to party. And speaking of which, I hear a street party has been organised, too. Get that bunting out!

There has been a real sense of community working together this year and we should all be proud of how our little town has commemorated the seventy-fifth anniversary of the D-Day landings.

Look out for a special picture edition of The Berecombe News to celebrate this most special of years.

Chapter One

Ashley cycled along Berecombe seafront, breathing in great gulps of salty Devon air. It was a detour from her flat to the Arts Workshop but, on a day like today, it was too good to miss. Making sure she didn't cycle too fast, as Bronte's lead was attached to the handlebars and she was running alongside, she stole a glance at the view. Now that the school holidays were over, most of the visitors she could see were retired, or young couples with pre-school-age children enjoying the beach and making the most of the blue skies and warm sunshine. The summer had been a series of long, hot, sunny days running into one another. And now, although it was early September, the weather was still balmy. It was possibly even better now that the shrill heat of July and August was softened by gentle breezes. As she slowly cycled she could hear the shrieks and giggles of children building sandcastles or paddling in Berecombe's safe, shallow waters.

Stopping to better enjoy the view, she checked on the little black poodle panting beside her. She was on her way to teach her first art class. Nerves suddenly hit; she hadn't taught for over two years. 'Ooh, Bronte, let's just hope I haven't forgotten how to do it!' she murmured. Lifting her face to the sun for a few luxurious seconds, she inhaled the soothing sea air and concentrated on slowing her breathing and calming herself down. The sea sparkled a dancing blue, pillowy clouds drifted and all around her were the happy sounds and intoxicating smells of a seaside town. Not for the first time she thanked her lucky stars that she'd ended up living in this quirky little town in east Devon. It had helped her heal, she'd made new friends and had a job she loved. And now she was about to take another step on the road to getting back to herself. No, she corrected. She was taking another leap into creating the new her! Her nerves were replaced by an enormous sense of well-being as with a grin she pushed off and headed for the Workshop.

An hour later, she faced the class in airy Studio One. It was a group of only nine and all women. Easels and chairs had been set up in a circle around a tableau of three white jugs sitting on some rich blue velvet with a bowl of vivid oranges. The colours popped and zinged and, along with the familiar scent of paint tickling her nostrils, took her straight back into her teaching days before her accident. She just hoped she could still do it. Forcing herself to relax, she remembered what Ken, her manager, had whispered to her on the way in. 'Remember, it's not like teaching schoolkids – they all want to be here. Or that's the theory.'

Ashley hoped so. At least her friend Beryl was here. The woman, dressed today in a bright pink linen smock and matching earrings, which contrasted with her silver pixie cut, gave her an encouraging wave as she sat down at one of the easels. Ashley smiled back. Beryl and Biddy, Berecombe's most notorious pensioners, had become two of her closest friends. She was particularly fond of Beryl. Biddy could be forthright and difficult, but Beryl was nothing but kindness and Ashley knew she was here to show moral support. If someone had told her two years ago that she'd be best buds with a couple of women well into their seventies, she would have laughed. But they'd become family – her family in Berecombe. She watched as the rest of the group settled. The only other woman she knew was Marti Cavendish from choir, who was chatting to a sleek middle-aged woman in expensive-looking white jeans. Ashley winced. Perhaps the first lesson might be about what was appropriate to wear in an art studio.

Ashley hesitated, wondering when the best time would be to bring the class to order. She couldn't believe how nervous she felt – her legs were trembling! She'd been teaching art all her working life, and even though Ken had said they differed from schoolchildren in that they'd paid to be here, that might well mean they'd be more demanding. Beryl caught her eye and winked. It gave her a little courage. No going back now.

Clearing her throat, she began to speak. 'If you could all face the front, then we can start.' No response, they were all too busy chatting. Oh God, it was going to be a disaster, wasn't it? What could she do? Taking a deep breath, Ashley dipped into her teacher's bag of tricks and summoned up her alter ego, the one she used to use to best effect with the tricky Year Nines on a wet Thursday afternoon. 'Right then,' she bellowed, making them all jump. 'Face this way, ladies, and we'll get going.' It worked. Even Marti stopped gossiping and faced the front. Teaching, Ashley suddenly remembered, was all about acting a part. Forcing yourself into the authority role and beaming out confident vibes even when, as now, it was the last thing you felt. She felt her shoulders loosen as she realised they were sitting up and paying attention. Out of the corner of her eye, she saw Beryl give her the thumbs-up. A rush of confidence flooded through her as she settled back into the old, familiar groove. She might not have taught for some time, but it was like riding a bike; she hadn't lost it after all.

Lowering the volume to a more conversational and friendly level, she said, 'We'll begin by introducing ourselves. I'll start. My name is Ashley Lydden. I've taught art for all of my teaching career, although I'll confess, this is my first class for a while.' Again, at the perimeter of her vision, she saw Beryl nod encouragingly. Forcing a smile, she added, 'I hope you'll forgive me if I'm a little rusty.' She was relieved to see that there were one or two sympathetic murmurs. They were on her side. Emboldened, she went on. 'You see, I had a car accident a while ago which meant I had to learn how to walk again.' A shocked sound rippled around the room. 'It also meant I couldn't stand for any length of time so I couldn't teach.' Ashley let out a breath. There was a time when she couldn't tell even her closest friends about the accident and now she was telling a room full of strangers. Realising how far she'd come in her recovery thrilled her. That and being back in an art studio and teaching. It was a wonderful feeling. She relaxed some more. She could do this! 'So, if I pull up a stool next to where you're working and sit on it peering over your shoulder, please don't be put off. It's just a more comfortable way for me to give you some feedback and tips.' Relieved laughter sounded and she felt her nerves calm. She'd definitely got them on side. Now she could take them with her on their learning journey. Oh, how she'd missed this. She hadn't actually known how much until this moment.

'After you've introduced yourselves, I'm going to set you a task so I can see how you work. It'll give me a good idea how to tailor the next lessons so I can best move you on. Remember, none of this is about competition.' At this Marti looked disappointed. 'It's about exploring and developing your own personal style and using a range of media and techniques. But most of all, it's about having fun!'

At the half-time break, Ken popped into Studio One to see how everything was going. 'Okay?' he asked.

'Think so,' she whispered. 'I remembered to do the health and safety and fire drill stuff, had a chat about wearing old clothes or bringing an old shirt, doled out the obligatory painting kit to those who thought it would be provided, and set them to a still life. Not very exciting but it gives me a chance to evaluate their skills. See what I'm working with.'

'Excellent idea. I watched a little of the session through the window just in case you needed me to jump in but there was no need. You handle them really well, Ashley, my friend. Just the right amount of encouragement and suggestion on how to improve. I didn't expect anything less.' As he saw Beryl approach, he added, 'I'll leave you to it. Looks like you've got it all under control. And, if it helps, imagine them all—'

'Naked. Yes, thanks, Ken. And it doesn't!'

He grinned, put up his hands in surrender and left.

'I've brought you a coffee,' Beryl said, handing over a mug. 'You're doing so well, my lovely. I've heard lots of compliments about how good a teacher you are.'

'Thanks, Beryl. I was so nervous at the start!'

'Absolutely no need and I can assure you it didn't show. We're all having a super time and learning lots.'

'I can't tell you how relieved I am that it's going well, and I *really* appreciate you coming along.' She glanced over to where the students had gathered around the hot water urn. 'I'm not sure if I ought to go and mingle at the tea table or leave them to bond as a group. If they were schoolkids, I'd leave them to it but—'

'Oh, they'll come over when they're ready. And in

Marti's case, it'll be to tell you how she narrowly missed out on getting into the Royal College of Art. She's already bored that nice lady wearing the white jeans.' Beryl winked, her wrinkles creasing into well-worn grooves. 'I'm amazed she's had time to fit everything she claims to have done into such a short life, especially as she only admits to thirty-nine.'

They laughed. Marti was well known for her boastful ways.

'I'm really enjoying this,' Beryl continued. 'Thanks for putting the class on. I'm missing choir ever since Petra left, so it fills a gap. And it's good to flex the old creative skills. If I have any.'

'I had a sneaky look when you popped to the loo. You've got talent, Beryl. And thank you for the kind words. If this goes well, I'll think about putting on more classes, maybe some in the evening for those not free during the day.'

'Excellent idea.'

'I miss choir, too,' Ashley said, as she sipped her coffee. 'I loved those fun sing-alongs, especially the *Grease* medleys. Always left in such a good mood. Really lifted the spirits.'

'Have you heard from Petra?'

Petra, Ashley's friend who had been running the choir, had recently skipped town unexpectedly.

'No. I imagine she's too busy. Touring the country with the band – going from town to town – can't leave much time spare.' Ashley supposed it was true, but she'd been disappointed that Petra hadn't rung. She'd thought they'd become close since she'd moved to Berecombe, and had considered Petra a good friend, so her sudden departure and radio silence ever since were hard for Ashley to process.

'Biddy's spitting feathers, she's that mad about the girl running off and leaving everyone in the lurch.'

'And no one wants to get on the wrong side of Biddy.'

'I have to agree. Although she's one of my dearest friends, I confess to treading warily around her.'

'At least the café is in safe hands with Tessa, Eleri and Zoe – though I know Petra's managerial skills are sorely missed. I think they're planning to carry on until Millie finds a new manager to take over Petra's job.'

'And at least Tess can use the kitchen to make her bread. I'm particularly fond of her walnut loaf. It's not ideal though. The girl really should have given poor Millie some notice. Sorry, Ashley, I know she's a friend of yours.'

'Was. I haven't heard from her since she left and she didn't tell me anything about going off to sing with the band.'

'How hurtful. And what about your nice young man? Is Eddie returning to Berecombe soon?'

'I hope so. He's hoping to spend some time in town when he gets back from the States and before he has to go to Bristol to start filming.'

'I'm so looking forward to this TV series he's doing. Folklore and myth! Right up my alley. Now, you must excuse me, I'm just going to say hello to one or two people.'

Ashley watched her go. Beryl's question about Eddie had made her insides go to mush in excitement. She couldn't wait to see him. As soon as they'd met, the attraction had been instant – and hot – but the relationship had been fraught with difficulties. Now, though, there was gentle hope on the horizon. Although not finding it easy, Ashley was gradually making peace with the fact that his ex-girlfriend was having his baby, and she had fully supported Eddie flying over to the States to be with Bree while she gave birth. They'd been in constant touch while he'd been in the US, but the time difference and his new baby made it difficult to talk.

Bree hadn't coped well after the birth, so they'd all gone to stay with Eddie's parents in Rockport, and he was leaving her and baby Hal there when he returned to the UK to make his new TV series. The set-up at Eddie's parents' sounded very cosy and Ashley was working hard at squashing down the jealousy; she felt very much the outsider – the other woman, even.

'Baby steps,' she muttered to herself, ignoring the irony. 'Baby steps.' This was one more thing she had to work on: coping with the fact that her new boyfriend had recently had a baby with another woman. Straightening her shoulders, she decided at this moment that she needed to concentrate on her job and wade in and get to know her class better. Heading over to the tea table, she went in search of more coffee and small talk.

Chapter Two

'Ashley? It's Petra.'

Ashley swung her legs off the sofa in shock, dislodging a grumbling Bronte. She was in her tiny flat and half-asleep, having indulged in a snooze before making supper. Holding the phone closer to her ear, she said, 'Hello, stranger.'

'Suppose I deserve that.'

'Well, yeah. You could have told me that you were planning on disappearing, Petra.' She heard a huge sigh at the other end of the line.

'I know. I got myself in a right old state about it. On one hand all I could see was my big break. Singing with the band and The Jenny WRENs to audiences who actually wanted to hear us, had *paid* to listen. It's all I've ever wanted to do, Ash. But then, there was the café... and Millie... and Berecombe. God, I love that town.'

'People are really missing choir.'

'I miss choir, too.'

Ashley heard a wobble in the voice. 'Beryl was saying at art class today how much she misses it. I do, too. I miss *you*, Petra.'

Petra gulped. 'I miss you, too, girlfriend. I can't believe you're being so nice to me. I don't deserve it. I've been meaning to ring for ages but kept putting it off. I didn't know how you'd feel about what I did. I bet the rest of Berecombe are baying for my blood, though.'

'Noah filled me in on a little bit of your childhood. About you being brought up in care. He said it's left you feeling as if you don't want to commit to anything, not on a permanent basis. He also explained how singing has been your dream for a long time. I sort of understand. I think. You could have talked to me, you know.'

'I know. But the way I grew up means you only have yourself to rely on. I don't find it easy to talk about myself.'

'Not even to your friends?'

'Am I still your friend, Ash?'

'Of course you are! I meant what I said, I really miss you. Place isn't the same without you.' She heard Petra blow her nose and gain some control.

'How's the caff?' she managed eventually.

'Millie's interviewing for a new café manager. In the meantime, Tessa, Eleri and Zoe are running it between them. Think Millie is hoping to get someone in before Zoe goes back to university in October.'

'I really messed them about, didn't I?'

'Well, yeah, to be honest, you did. But you know what folk in this town are like, they'll forgive you. When you come back all will be forgotten.'

'Even by Biddy?'

'Ah. Can't vouch for Biddy, although she might surprise you. She was amazing when we did the tea dance.'

'The tea dance! How did it go?'

Ashley thought back to the afternoon she and Petra had planned together as a tribute to the GIs who were staying in town as part of the D-Day seventy-fifth anniversary, and smiled. They'd had great fun working together on what food to serve, what music to play and who to invite, but Petra had left town before the event. 'It was a triumph. Your menu worked a treat, everyone danced and the sun shone. You would have been proud of how everyone came together to make it a success. But tell me about your tour. How's it all going? Hard work?'

'I'm knackered. Thought running the café was hard work but this is crazy. We spend hours in a van, all huddled up, get to some crappy digs, rehearse in a freezing-cold venue, perform, go to bed and then do it all over again the next day. The glamour of showbiz!'

'And you love it.'

'And I love it. One hundred per cent.' There was a pause. 'What's that scrabbling, chewing sort of a noise I can hear? Have you got mice?'

'It's Bronte, my poodle. She's chewing on the new toy I bought her on the way back from art class.'

'You've got a poodle? How did that come about?'

Ashley explained about the owner going into care and not being able to take her dog with her. 'So I adopted Bronte. Wouldn't be without her. She slept in her bed during the art class and was as good as gold. I was so proud of her.'

'She sounds lovely. I love Biddy's dog Elvis, so I can imagine she's just as cute. And what's this about an art class? Are you taking a class? Shouldn't think you need to.'

'Not taking, I'm *teaching* it.'

'Oh, Ash, you star, you. You go, girl! That's a huge step forward. I'm so pleased for you. Oh, I wish I was there to give you a great big hug.'

'Big hugs coming down the line right back atcha. I absolutely love it. Can't say it's as glam as your life but oh, Petra, it's so good to be back doing it again. I'm only doing four hours a week for now, but I'll build up if I can.'

'That's so great. How did the first class go?'

'Well, okay, I think.' Ashley felt a surge of pride as she remembered the comments from the students as they left. 'No, I *know* it went well. I got some really good feedback afterwards. I was nervous beforehand – thought I was going to be sick at one point and nearly backed out – but as soon as I started, it all began to come back. There's so much joy in pointing people towards how they could improve a skill. Only these are adults and not squelchy adolescents. Some of them are quite demanding and one really knows her art history. I definitely had to up my game but, you know what, I thoroughly enjoyed the challenge.'

'Sounds like you're getting your life back on track. I'm so pleased for you, hon.'

'Thanks. I think I am. I feel like things are slotting into place. Physically, I feel so much better, and after this first class, the confidence is coming back too. I really enjoyed it, but I have to confess it's exhausted me. Must be all the nervous energy I used up! I was having a snooze on the sofa when you rang. Not used to being on my feet so much. Plus, I've got Marti Cavendish in the class so she's keeping me on my toes, so to speak.'

'Not Marti! The opera star?'

'And now apparently Royal College of Art entrant. Her talents have no—'

'Beginning!' they said simultaneously and laughed.

'It's so good to talk to you, Petra.' Ashley felt a swell of emotion for her friend. She'd only got to know Petra since moving to Berecombe but they'd quickly become good friends and she'd been lonely since she left. 'You will keep in touch from now on, won't you? Oh, and ring my big coz Noah, will you? He'd love to hear from you. I know you and he had something going on between you before you went away, and I think he'd like to make it something more. Ooh, hang on, Bronte's barking. I've got to go, there's someone at the door. Ring me again when you can. I still haven't told you about me and Eddie.'

'Don't tell me things have finally moved on between you two?'

'Okay, I'm coming,' Ashley called towards the door. 'Bronte, stop barking. Look, I've got to go, the dog's going nuts. Ring me again, or you won't hear about what's happening with Eddie,' she threatened jokingly.

'Will do!' Petra giggled. 'Bye, honeybun.'

Ashley clicked off the call, grabbed Bronte by the collar and opened the front door. This was the first time someone had rung the doorbell since she'd had the dog and it had obviously unsettled her. Picking her up, she straightened to see a tall man standing there. A tall man with a suntan and a familiar wide grin.

'Hi, Ash,' Eddie said. 'So, this is Bronte!'

Chapter Three

'Eddie!' Excitement at seeing him after so long overshot any inhibition and she grabbed him and hugged him tight, the little poodle still in her arms.

'Think something's coming between us, kiddo.' He looked down in alarm. 'And it's growling.'

'I probably squashed her.' Ashley stared at Bronte, stricken. 'Did I squish you, little one? Come on, I'll find you a Bonio.'

'Do I get one too?' Eddie asked, amused.

'Do you eat dog biscuits?' she said over her shoulder. 'Or would you settle for a beer?' He followed her into the sitting room, and she busied herself with the tin of biscuits and settling the dog in her basket. As ever, Eddie's bulk dominated the tiny space, and it made her self-conscious.

'You know what I'd really like?'

'What's that?'

'A cup of good old British tea.'

'I think I can manage that.' Moving into the kitchen, she washed her hands and switched on the kettle. 'When did you get in?'

'Got the red eye into Bristol, headed straight into a meeting for my show and then drove here.' He yawned hugely. 'Jeez though, flying this direction always knocks me out. Tried to sleep on the plane but I never can.'

She took out two mugs. 'And how's everything at home, with... erm... Bree and the baby?'

He scrubbed an exhausted hand over his eyes. 'Yeah. Okay. All good. Bree's staying with Mom until she feels stronger. Mom's loving having a baby to look after.'

'It must have been awful leaving Hal.'

'It was. Yeah.'

There was something off about his tone but Ashley put it down to jetlag and decided not to pursue the topic just now. Changing gears, she said, 'I've just been speaking to Petra on the phone.'

'Oh? Good. How's she doing?'

While she made the tea, Ashley filled him in on everything Petra had told her. Bringing the tray over to where he was sitting, she put it on the table in front of the sofa and sat on the floor. It reminded her of when

Eddie had first called at the flat all those months ago. She recalled the almost instant physical attraction she'd felt to him and smiled. It had been so uncomplicated back then when her only concern had been the speed and intensity of her feelings.

Bronte, having scoffed the biscuit, decided she wanted to investigate the visitor so jumped onto the sofa and sniffed Eddie.

'Hey there, little one,' he crooned, holding out his hand. 'See, I'm not so scary.' Bronte whickered a little, turned round and stuck her bottom up in the air.

Ashley laughed. 'Believe it or not, that means she likes you.'

Eddie scratched the dog's rump and Bronte, in ecstasies, wiggled round and cuddled into him.

'There you go, friend for life.'

'Feels good to have a dog next to me again.'

'You must miss yours,' Ashley said softly. Eddie's elderly Labrador, Bowie, had been put to sleep a few months previously whilst in Bree's care.

He glanced up, his hazel eyes full of emotion. 'I did. Still do, I guess. Not as much as I've missed you though, Ash.' Bronte, as though sensing his anguish, settled on his lap. As he cuddled the dog, his face was shuttered but Ashley could hear the pain in his voice. 'I really felt for Bree having to make the decision to have him put to sleep. It's a tough enough thing to do for your own dog but when you're looking after someone else's it's even harder.'

'I'm sure she did what she felt she had to.'

'Yeah, I guess.' He shoved an exhausted hand through his hair, making it untidy. 'It's all been hard, Ash. God knows it's not how I saw me having a child – getting my ex pregnant by accident when we'd split up. I feel constantly torn in two. I was desperate to get back to you, but it was hell leaving Hal.'

'It must have been.' Ashley felt a pang of the familiar jealousy and tried to repress it. She needed to learn to accept baby Hal. 'When are you hoping to get back and see them again?'

He gave her a hard, swift glance. 'See Hal. It's only Hal I want to see, not Bree. And, much as I long to be with my son in the States, this is where I want to be. I want to be with you, Ash, here, in the UK. It's where my work is now.' His eyes flickered with emotion as his gaze intensified. 'It's where my heart is, too.'

This was how her life would be from now on, Ashley thought. If she built a relationship with Eddie, Hal – and to some extent, Bree – would always be there in his life too. And it wouldn't change even once Hal was out of the baby stage. She wondered if it would get slightly easier, though, when Hal was older. He'd be able to stay with his father independently, maybe even come and live in the UK with them. But that all seemed a long way off. A flash of understanding seared her brain. However hard it was for her, it must be doubly so for Eddie. He'd miss so much of his son growing up. Breath snatched in her throat. He was willing to give all that up because he wanted to live in England and to be with her. It was some sacrifice.

'Eddie, I—' she began.

'Ashley, if you don't come over here and kiss me, I'm not going to be responsible for my actions. Get here now. I gotta prove to you it's not Bree I want.'

'But we have things to talk through.'

'Yes, we do,' he agreed wearily. 'But not right now. Right now I just need to hold you. I'm aching to hold you.'

Ashley pulled herself up and slid onto the sofa next to him, which, as always, sagged in the middle and threw them together. Eddie didn't move. She looked directly into his eyes. 'Well,' she said, with a shy smile, 'what are you waiting for? I'm here.'

He groaned, slipped a hand around the back of her neck and pulled her close. Bronte jumped off his lap and slunk to her basket to watch the proceedings with interest. Eddie sank his face into Ashley's hair and inhaled. 'You smell so damn good,' he whispered. 'You always did. Did you know your scent comes to me in my dreams? It haunts me.'

His low voice, pulsing with need, sent thrills running through her body. She shifted closer, resting her head on his shoulder, and they sat close together, content for the moment to simply listen to one another breathe.

After a long time, Ashley asked quietly, 'Did you make any progress with your grandfather's story when you were back home?' Eddie seemed such a huge part of her life now, it was strange to think it was only a few months ago that he'd come to Berecombe to find out more about his GI relative who had been billeted in the town in the months before D-Day. It was how they had come together. She had been planning the funeral for another war hero – a local man, Jimmy Larcombe – and Eddie thought Jimmy might have known his grandfather.

Eddie groaned. 'It's like pulling teeth. So slow! I got through to some guy at the regimental headquarters. He said he'd do the research, send on any paperwork or records he had, but it would take time.'

'I'm sorry.'

'Guess I'm no further forward than I was back in February. I'll just have to wait to see what they come up with.' He shifted away and reached into his pocket. 'I brought this back though. Thought you might like to see it. It's his dog tag. Mom thought I ought to have it. She had it put on a chain if I ever wanted to wear it, but it didn't seem right somehow.' He handed it over.

Ashley took it, the cold links of the chain slithering between her trembling fingers. It was small, metal and oblong, the letters and numbers worn smooth and almost indecipherable. She didn't think she would be able to wear it either if she was in Eddie's shoes. This had been around a soldier's neck when he'd gone into battle – and in Eddie's grandfather's case, into some of the most brutal fighting of World War Two. 'Fascinating.' She handed it back, shivering a little.

He put it back in his pocket. 'It resonates, doesn't it? Oh, Ash, I'm sorry. I didn't mean to upset you,' he said, seeing the emotion in her eyes. 'Hey, come here. I'm sorry,' he repeated. 'Let's forget about all that.' He hugged her close and then, lifting her chin with the tip of his finger, he outlined her mouth, frowning as he did so, as if trying to commit its shape to memory. Running his hand over her face he traced her eyebrows, the contours of her cheekbones. He found the scar from her accident behind her ear and tipped her head gently sideways to trace it with his lips, his touch so delicate and needy, her breath hitched. His lips trailed over her jaw, remembering the sensitive part of her neck, and his fingers found her collar bone and the swell of her breast.

And then he groaned again, and their mouths found one another and they kissed. They were tentative at first, exploring, hardly daring to believe they could, after all this time. Then Ashley flung her arms around his neck and pulled him in close, relishing the weight of him against her. The mood shifted and built into an urgent longing.

Eddie unzipped her jeans and slid his hand under the denim. Ashley's head fell back, her eyes closed as she concentrated on the deliciousness of the skin-on-skin touch. She wanted him so much. Through the hot fug of her need, she pictured them sprawled naked on her bed. Eddie's hand skimmed hotly over her hip. Naked. They'd be naked. She froze. All desire fled.

He picked up on the sudden change in mood instantly. 'Too soon? Too much?' He backed off and gazed into her eyes. 'What's wrong, Ash?' Seeing her distress, he caressed her cheek. 'Hey, baby, what's wrong?'

'I—' She faltered. How could she explain? Especially as she'd shown no such inhibition the time she'd launched herself at him outside the theatre. But she'd had clothes on then.

He sat back, gently tidying her shirt. 'It's too soon for you, isn't it? Maybe we should sit back, take it easy, have that talk. Come here.' He pulled her back to him once more, resting her head on his shoulder, banding his arms around her. Gradually their breathing returned to normal.

'I need to tell you something.'

'Shoot, kiddo. I'm all ears.' His hand stroking her hair soothed.

'I'm ugly, Eddie.'

Chapter Four

'I have scars,' she continued. 'As well as the one on my face, I have scars from the surgery following the accident on my hips and across my abdomen.'

'Aw, honey, of course you've got scars. No one could have gone through what you have and not have them.' He stiffened. Holding her so he could see her face, he added, 'Did you think that would change how I feel? Do you think me so shallow?'

'They're not pretty.'

He shook his head vehemently. 'Your scars are you. They are what make you you.' He touched his hand to her cheek again. 'You'll never be ugly to me. You're beautiful. In fact, you're the most beautiful woman I've ever met. I thought that the very first moment I saw you sitting on the bench on the prom. All that glorious hair blowing in the breeze, your tongue sticking out as you concentrated on your painting, and then, when you took off your sunglasses, I saw those eyes. Eyes a man could drown in, Ash. But you're beautiful inside too. You're kind and funny, clever and talented, and, hey, you underestimate yourself shockingly. When I handed over your painting kit and you got all prickly about it going back in the right order, I was sunk. No way back.' He laughed a little. 'Just call me a sucker for a woman with talent.' He sobered. 'And I know I'm a lot to take on, what with Hal being in the picture. I know that's hard for you.' He shrugged. 'I'm not going to lie; this is killing me. I want to rip your clothes off and have you right here, right now, but we can stay like this if you like. It'll kill me' – he grinned – 'but we can take this at any pace that suits you. I'm in your hands.'

Ashley gulped. In the soft light from the lamp, he was the most beautiful man she'd ever seen. And the kindest. 'It's just that... I mean, I do want you. I'll rephrase that, I'm desperate for you.'

He smiled. 'Good to hear.'

'But you'd be the first man to see me naked since the accident.' She bit her lip. 'I didn't think it would bother me. I've nearly got used to them, forget they're even there most of the time, until I catch a glimpse in the shower.' She shuddered. 'Then they bring back memories. Of the accident.'

'Of course they do but that'll change. Give it time. It's only been a couple of years, hasn't it? It takes time.'

'I stare at them and think I'll never be the woman I was before.'

'You're not the woman you were. You're better. You're the woman I've fallen in love with. Because I do love you, Ash. You must know that.'

Ashley stared at him. She nodded. She tried to find the same words to say back but there was still so much about her that he didn't know. He might not be as free with his declarations when he knew the truth. She reached for her mug of tea, now stone cold, to give her time to think. There were things that needed to be said. Nothing between her and Eddie could progress until then. But still she couldn't tell him the most significant thing. Instead, she settled for sorting out a misunderstanding. 'I don't know if I said this clearly enough but when we were on the steam train, back in the summer, I was annoyed with Petra being in a mood and I think you got caught in the crossfire. There really wasn't anything between me and Jake Tremayne.' Jake was an artist who had exhibited at the Arts Workshop. He was outrageously flirtatious and charismatic, and Ashley had almost fallen under his spell. At the first night of his exhibition, Eddie had caught them on the brink of a kiss.

'I know.'

She twisted to look up at him.

'I could see you were in a blue about something that night, at his exhibition opening. I just didn't know what. And call me arrogant but I knew you couldn't feel like that about him when you'd kissed me like you did at choir. Jeez, Ash, do you know what you did to me that night?'

Ashley's face flushed warm at the memory of how she'd been overcome by her feelings for Eddie and things had got decidedly heated one night in the courtyard outside Berecombe's Regent Theatre.

'But al fresco sex?' He grinned. 'How can I say this? It's never been my style. Prefer a nice comfortable bed. But you were coming on strong, girl, not long after telling me all you wanted was friendship. I could see that wasn't going to be on the cards, not the way you launched yourself at me.' He picked up his mug, grimaced at the cold contents and put it down again. 'When I saw you with Jake,' he said, carefully, 'guess you could say I was confused. Pissed. And oh so jealous.' At her quiver he added, 'Oh boy, was I jealous. You looked so lovely that night and his hands were all over you.

Didn't want to cause a scene so I left. After a few choice words, of course.'

'Which I think I deserved.' She pulled a face.

'What were you trying to do with him?'

Ashley sighed. 'Oh, who knows. You weren't the only one who was confused. Think I was trying to blot you out, see if I could distract myself with someone less complicated.'

'Less complicated? Jake Tremayne?' His lips twisted in humour.

'I know, I know. I wasn't thinking straight. You'd got me so confused I couldn't see reason for the lust.'

'Did I now?' he asked, looking pleased with himself.

She risked a giggle. 'You can stop looking so smug. I've never thought of myself as being a particularly sexual person but after that kiss at choir, all I could think about was getting laid, preferably by you.'

Eddie roared. 'That's something coming out of an English mouth. Say it again.'

'What, getting laid?'

'Oh baby, you don't know what that's doing to me.' He laced a hand through her hair and kissed her.

She reached for him, the need for his body setting her nerves on fire. It was getting hot and steamy again, but she pushed him off. 'There's something I need to tell you first.'

He flicked his hair out of his eyes. 'Something else?'

'Yes, and I need to tell you this now, while I've got the courage.'

He shifted away from her. 'Sounds serious.'

'It is. Or could be. Or has the potential to be. It explains a lot of things. A lot of how I've reacted to you, to the news of Bree and especially the baby.'

'Okay.' He leaned back against the sofa. Spreading his arms, he invited her in again and held her against him.

Ashley hoped what she was about to tell him wouldn't mean the end of them, but she had to be honest with him; he deserved as much. And knowing the truth about her was the only way she could see them having any kind of future. 'You know I was in this accident.'

He stroked her hair. 'Yeah. The car smash. I know. It sounds nightmarish and you were badly injured. But you're all healed up now?' His hand stilled. 'I haven't done anything to hurt you, have I?' he asked anxiously. 'Just now? When we were kissing?'

'No.' She shook her head against his chest. 'No, you didn't hurt me. I don't think you ever could. You're too nice a man.'

He groaned. 'That "nice" word. Kiss of death for any man. You know we want to be thought of as alpha-male-sexy and strong, don't you? Next thing you'll be telling me you just want to be friends again.' There was a pause and then he said, panicked, 'God, you don't, do you?'

'No.' Ashley took a deep breath. It was now or never. He might not want to be with a woman who couldn't give him more children, but she had to tell him. 'At the last check-up, my consultant suggested that... that...'

'Yes? Jeez, Ashley, you're okay, aren't you?' He took her face in his hands and gazed into her eyes. 'I mean, you're not sick or anything?'

'I'm perfectly fine. Apart from an occasional balance issue and a limp when I'm tired, I'm nearly all healed. I don't even use my stick most of the time now.'

Eddie relaxed back. 'You had me worried there.'

'It's just that there's one thing the consultant mentioned, which can be a common complication in women with pelvic injuries.'

'Which is?' His arm around her shoulders tightened.

'There's a possibility, although it's not certain yet, that I won't be able to—' She swallowed, her heart beating wildly. 'Won't be able to have children.'

There was a silence while he digested the news. He blew out a huge breath. Dropping a kiss on her hair, he said eventually, 'No wonder you were freaked when I told you Bree was having a baby. All makes sense now.' After another pause, he added, 'God, Ash, this must have been hell for you.' Gathering her up in his arms, he added, 'My poor love. My poor, poor darling.'

They sat in silence for a while, the only sound being Bronte's light breathing as she slept.

'How do you feel about the news?' he finally asked.

'It's a lot to process and it's still uncertain but the consultant said it might be difficult to carry a baby full term or give birth' – Ashley felt her face heat – 'erm... vaginally. Also, we Lyddens have twins in our genes. My dad and Noah's are identical twins. One reason we're so close, perhaps.'

'And having twins is an extra complication?' She felt him nod in response to his own question. 'Yes, I can see that.' He kissed her hair again. 'Just wish you'd told me sooner, kiddo. There's me thinking there was something about *me* that you couldn't stand, apart from the Bree situation, of course.'

She stroked a hand across his shirt, feeling his heart quicken and enjoying the solid warmth of his body. 'No, it was never about you. Never! It's something I'm still coming to terms with myself. I would've told you before but I couldn't get past the fact that Bree had given you something I might never be able to. You talked about being jealous earlier. So was I. It was eating me up, making me mad, irrational. It certainly made me behave badly and especially badly towards you.' She looked up. 'I can't tell you how sorry I am for that.'

'Hey, nothing to be sorry for.' He traced a delicate finger over the scar on her face. 'You've been through so much. You met a guy. You liked the guy. Then he drops the bombshell that his ex is having his baby. Took me long enough to get my head around the idea. I can't imagine how it must have been for you.' He tucked a finger under her chin, forcing her to meet his gaze. 'I wanted to break it to you gently, on the night of the charity ball, but Bree steamed ahead in her usual way. Think she enjoyed spilling the beans.'

'I think she did.'

'I gave her hell afterwards. I was so pissed at her.'

'Did you?' Ashley asked, quietly pleased.

'Yeah. You could say whatever scales were left dropped from my eyes in that moment. She's always been one for the dramatic, for playing games, and she doesn't care who gets hurt in the process. Took me a while to figure that out but I got there in the end. I really saw her for who she is. She knows it, too.' He kissed her lightly on the nose. 'You do know it's most definitely over between me and her, don't you?'

'Yes, I do.' Ashley shifted and looked him in the face. All she saw was kindness and concern. It made what she was about to say even harder. 'It's just that' – she bit her lip – 'knowing I might not be able to have children and knowing how desperately you want more, I'm not sure there's any future for a relationship between us.'

Shock sparked his eyes into darkness. 'Oh, Ashley.' He sighed as he slid his hands to either side of her face to bring her in for a kiss. A long, sweetly tender kiss. 'Don't you know me better than that by now, honey? I'd rather be with you and take the chance of not having more children, than be with someone else. *Anyone else*, you hear? We'll take it slow and deal with whatever comes our way when it does. Trust me?'

She nodded, her relief at finally having told him leaving her weak. 'I trust you.'

Chapter Five

For the next few days, Ashley wandered around
with a beaming smile and a light heart. It was
liberating having told Eddie the truth. She hadn't known
what a burden it had been until it was lifted. He'd been
gracious about it all and she felt closer to him than ever
before; that a relationship with him was really going to
work. They'd made more tea, ordered in a takeaway, and
had talked long into the night. She'd drunk in his very
American confidence that if one consultant said one
thing, they'd find another, but wasn't sure it worked that
way in the NHS. They'd held one another close until the
conversation faltered and she'd looked up to see him fast
asleep, jetlag having finally caught up. Tucking a blanket
over him, she'd sat on the floor and watched him as he

slept. Sleep stole the worry puckers from around his eyes and smoothed his skin; he looked younger and at peace. He'd left early the next morning to head back to Bristol, promising to be back for Ruby's birthday street party, if not before. Ashley accepted this was how it was going to be: passionate moments snatched in between their work commitments. He'd told her not to worry. That although he'd have to go away, he'd always return, and that Berecombe would be the still centre of peace he'd come back to. And when he kissed her goodbye, she was filled with such a rush of starry happiness and well-being she thought anything could be possible.

Being happy gave her a sunny energy, which she ploughed into her teaching and enjoying everything that September in Berecombe could offer. Biddy's houseguest, Ruby, would soon celebrate her ninety-second birthday and Ashley was thrilled when her idea to hold a surprise party was met with enthusiasm. She and Biddy quickly set about organising it. It seemed the least she could do; Ruby had become an unlikely but dear friend. Ashley had been recording her memories of being a World War Two evacuee for Noah's Living Memories Exhibition at the town's museum where he was director. Ruby's stories of being a young girl in love with an American GI had captivated them all. Her heartbreak when she'd become pregnant by Chet, her soldier sweetheart, only to lose the baby, had held Ashley enthralled and had forged an indelible bond between them.

One of the highlights of the autumn schedule was the film festival. Organised by the patron of the Regent Theatre, Mike Love, as part of the commemorations for the seventy-fifth anniversary of D-Day, it was causing great excitement in a town that had long since lost its only cinema. On the night that the theatre was showing a double bill of Fred Astaire and Ginger Rogers films she met up with Beryl, Biddy and her long-suffering husband Arthur, and their granddaughter Zoe. They brought along Ruby, too.

'The dress code said nineteen-thirties glamour,' Beryl said with glee as they met up by the bar. 'And you know me, I love a chance to get dressed up!'

'You look wonderful,' Ashley replied, leaning forward and kissing her. 'That slinky silver dress is fabulous.'

Beryl grinned and flicked her skirts to show them off. 'The charity shop's finest.'

'It must have done a roaring trade. By the time I got there, this feather boa was the only thing I could find.'

'Well, better to make some effort than none at all. Can I buy you a martini, my lovely?'

Ashley giggled. 'A martini?'

'The bar is doing them as a special. In the proper glasses, too.'

'In that case, it would be rude to refuse.'

'Two martinis coming right up, complete with green olives. And I have to say, they've tried hard with this old place to make it look as glamorous as possible.'

'I agree.' Ashley looked round. The dark, slightly crumbling interior of the theatre had been transformed. Long fringes of silver tinsel hung from the walls and shimmered with movement in the draught of people passing. Someone had loaned three enormous spotlights, which looked as if they'd come straight from the set of a black-and-white movie, and posters of iconic films had been framed in silver and hung up. There were even three palm trees in pots. It didn't quite disguise the shabbiness, but it was all frivolous and great fun. Along with most of the audience turning up in some semblance of fancy dress, if you squinted hard and used a great deal of imagination you could almost picture yourself at a Hollywood premiere.

As Beryl turned to go, Biddy tapped Ashley on the shoulder. 'Coming through,' she yelled and followed her friend to the bar.

'Step-gran's on a mission,' Zoe said with a giggle.

'She wants to get a round of drinks in before they run out of martinis.'

'Hi, Zoe, you look great.'

The girl preened a little. She was dressed in a black-tie trouser suit and had her hair gelled back, with a kiss curl plastered onto her forehead. Holding up a long cigarette holder, she grinned. 'Channelling Berlin *Cabaret* chic. The Drama Soc put it on at uni last year and I've been in love with Sally Bowles ever since. Grandad's come as a gangster. Have you seen him? He's over there getting Ruby to her seat. Old Rube's looking good, too.'

Ashley looked over to where Arthur was solicitously putting Ruby into a seat at the end of a row near the front of the theatre. 'He's such a kind man.'

'He is. Kinder than a very kind thing.'

'And he probably has to put up with a fair bit, married to Biddy.'

'He loves her,' Zoe said simply. 'And she loves him very much. They're poles apart in terms of personality and Biddy has more baggage than Paddington's left luggage but it's pure love between them. Besides, you don't get to choose who you fall in love with, do you? It might be someone so different to you they seem like they're off another planet or have stuff going on you think you'll never be able to deal with. Love is strong enough. Don't they say it conquers all?

Well, my grandad and Biddy are living proof.' She shrugged and suddenly became a twenty-something student again. 'When I've told my mates at uni they've got the ick at two old wrinklies getting the hots but I think it's cool.'

Ashley observed Zoe. The girl was frighteningly self-possessed and mature beyond her years, and her words had made Ashley pause. Would love alone be enough for herself and Eddie? Would she be able to overcome Hal and Bree being in his life? She fervently hoped so. She hoped she'd begin to see Hal as her son one day, too. He might be the only child she'd have. 'What about you?' she asked the girl. 'Anyone on the scene?'

'Nah. One or two flings with tourists this summer but been too busy working at the caff.'

'It's great that you, Tessa and Eleri are running Millie Vanilla's between you. I know Millie appreciates it. She was stuck when Petra left so suddenly.'

'No biggie.' Zoe shrugged again. 'I've worked there off and on for yonks. Tessa uses the kitchen to bake her bread and she's selling it in the café so it's a win-win for her. I love working with Eleri, too. I swear she hypnotises the punters. She's magic.'

'Quite literally, some say. I've heard the rumours that she's part mermaid.'

'I know, right?' Zoe's eyes went huge. 'I keep trying to get a look at her feet to see if she's got webbed toes.'

Ashley laughed. 'Is she coming tonight?'

'No. Having a cosy night in with her best beloved Alex. Running the hotel on top of working at the café means she's knackered. Millie should be here though. She's got the night off from being a mummy to the gorge baby Bobbie.'

'It'll be nice to see her. Oh, here come the martinis.' Biddy and Beryl bustled up to them both carrying a tray laden with cone-shaped glasses. 'Ooh, thank you,' Ashley said, as she took one. 'I'm not sure I've ever had a martini before. You're looking splendid, Biddy.' She was. Dressed in a bright green low-waisted silk dress, with long strings of pearls around her neck and elbow-length gloves, she looked the part of a 1930s film star. Not for the first time Ashley pondered the extent of Biddy's wardrobe.

Biddy looked her up and down. 'You've got to make an effort, haven't you? You could have asked if you wanted to borrow something, you know, young Ashley.'

Ashley plucked at her pink feather boa self-consciously and sipped her cocktail. 'Thank you,' she mumbled, feeling thoroughly chastened. 'I'll remember next time.'

Beryl rescued her. 'I have to say you're looking very well these days, Ashley.' She turned to the others. 'She's doing a wonderful job teaching the art classes. The pupils are all singing her praises.'

Biddy hmphed and said with a gleam in her eye, 'Not sure that's what's causing Ashley's glow.'

'Hello, my lovelies.' Millie breezed up to the group. 'Look who I found loitering outside.'

'Hey there,' Eddie said. 'Well, looky-here. All my favourite people in one room.'

'Eddie!' Ashley passed Zoe her glass and flung her arms around his neck. 'I didn't think you were going to make it!'

He lifted her up and spun her around. Then, putting her down, he sneezed. 'I got feathers up my nose. What's with the boa?'

'Fancy dress in honour of Fred and Ginger,' she said, holding onto him and smiling up. 'Why didn't you tell me you were coming?'

'Last-minute reprieve. The shoot finished up early, which is apparently unheard of in telly land.' He grinned, the deep groove of his dimple appearing in his cheek. 'How could I miss the chance of seeing *Top Hat* and *Shall We Dance* on a big screen?' He hummed the tune to 'They Can't Take That Away from Me' while staring intently into her eyes.

From somewhere near her Ashley heard Beryl sigh and say, 'Oh my, how romantic!'

'Come on then,' she heard Biddy say. 'Stop gawping, give them some privacy. If we don't get to our seats now all the best ones will have gone. Beryl, woman, stop snivelling and shift your stumps.'

Ashley ignored them. She was too busy enjoying the sensation of dissolving in the intensity of Eddie's gaze. It might have been the effects of the martini but she felt her feelings for the man shift from love into something beyond that she couldn't and didn't need to name. She simply wanted to bask in it. As the others made their way to their seats, she almost made a declaration. Deciding it probably wasn't the time or place but melting at the romance, she put her head onto one side coquettishly. 'You might change your mind about wanting to see *Shall We Dance*.'

'Why's that?' he asked, still smiling, still gazing at her intently, his hazel eyes darkening with emotion.

'It happens to feature the song "Let's Call the Whole Thing Off".'

Eddie reached down and pulled her to him again. Nuzzling into her neck, he whispered, laughing, 'Potato, Pota-to, I don't care how you pronounce it. I just want to make fries with you.'

Giggling, she responded, 'You say fries, I say chips.' And, as the implication caught, she gasped and added, 'But yes, I want to make fries with you, too!'

'Come on, guys. Sorry to break you up.' It was Millie. 'Much as I'd love to take credit for this most recent love match, I've three fresh martinis here and I'm a new mummy on a mission to have a baby-free good time. Let's go watch some films.'

Chapter Six

Biddy's suggestion that they hold a street party for Ruby's birthday was genius. The road that ran parallel to the promenade had been partially closed due to some roadworks in the town, so it made sense to take advantage, and the weather had settled into long, golden days of gentle sunshine. There was also the fact that Biddy had argued they needed to celebrate the culmination of a year's community effort and why not have Victor, the one remaining GI, and birthday girl Ruby as guests of honour? Ashley had obtained some funding from the forbiddingly efficient Tash, who ran the town's estate agency, Biddy had unravelled what was possibly seventy-odd years' worth of bunting, and businesses all along the seafront had promised trestle tables and chairs. With the trusty crew from the WI, it was going to be a real community event. Ashley had ordered a specially made birthday cake and was looking forward to giving something back to Ruby, who had been so generous with her story for the living history project at the Berecombe Museum. Even the reappearance of Ruby's daughter, Serena, hadn't dampened her mood. The woman seemed a little mellowed, maybe due to the effect of her recent Italian holiday, or perhaps it was being cosseted at The Henville Hotel, with Ruby resolutely staying put at Biddy and Arthur's.

The morning of the party dawned, thankfully dry and warm. There was already a long line of tables in place along Berecombe promenade, which for once didn't have a queue of cars trying to park, and Biddy was loudly supervising the placing of more. Local farmer George Small had even donated straw bales from his farm for those who wanted somewhere more casual to perch.

'I've a surprise in store for Ruby,' Ashley's cousin Noah said as he adjusted the patriotically coloured bunting. He clambered down from the stepladder he'd been standing on.

'What's that?' she asked.

Noah tapped his nose. 'Now that would be telling, wouldn't it, coz?'

'You can be infuriating sometimes.'

'But you still love me. And speaking of which, is it love between you and our delightful American friend?'

'Could be. Or heading that way,' she replied blithely as she opened up a box of serviettes.

Noah executed a mock swoon. 'You don't mean… you've told him The Big Secret and it all went okay?'

'I did and he's fine with it.' She frowned. 'In fact, he was a lot kinder than you're being at the moment.' Snatching up a tea towel, she flicked it at him.

'Ouch!' he roared.

'Make yourself useful and lay out the cups and saucers on the table next to the tea urn.'

He clattered about with the crockery. 'I'm over the moon for you, Ash. Although it's not before time. So, how's it going to work? Between you and Eddie, I mean?'

'The usual way, I expect. He will insert his—'

'La-la-la!' Noah exclaimed, putting his hands over his ears. 'I do not want to hear this.' He picked up the tea towel and flicked it back at her. 'As you well knew, I *meant* how are you two going to conduct a relationship with him filming this TV show all over the West Country and then jetting off to visit his son?'

She screwed up her face. 'I don't know. We haven't discussed it. But people manage, don't they? Millie was telling me earlier that her friend Clare has an Italian lover

53

and they spend six months in Italy and six months in Devon. I'm coming round to the idea that I'd like to be part of his son's life, help bring him up, so I'd probably need to travel to the States too.'

He turned to stare at her intently. 'But what about your job? Your teaching? You're just getting started again.' He spread his hands to the glory that was the sparkling sea and golden sands of Berecombe seafront. 'You've made a home here, got settled, made friends. Would you really want to give all that up?'

Ashley swallowed. She hadn't thought of it that way. 'No. You know how much I love it here.'

'I suppose it might be better had Eddie stayed teaching at the university. At least he'd be in one place and Exeter's commutable.'

'He's told me he can't maintain his lecturing commitments and fulfil his filming so he's not going to renew his university contract.' She paused, the enormity of the situation becoming a reality. And there was she, thinking the only complication in any relationship with Eddie was his son with his ex. 'It's early days but maybe we'll get a flat or a house somewhere, as a base.'

'Aw, Ash, don't move out from the flat. I like having you downstairs.'

'It's not very big, Noah. I mean, it's fine for me and Bronte but it gets a bit cramped when Eddie's there.'

'The Dimmocks, my lovely landlords, will be sad to see you go. Said you've been the best tenant they've had.' He smoothed out a wrinkle in the white paper table covering in front of him. 'And I can't see you as the sort of woman patiently waiting at home until her lord and master decides to return from his hunting and gathering.'

'Look,' she said, losing patience, 'Eddie and I have only just got together. We haven't even been on a proper date yet. We'll take it slow and sort it out between us.' Somehow, she added silently. 'And can I remind you that you're the one who's been pressurizing me into thinking of Eddie as a soulmate? So back off.'

'Okay. Okay.' He shrugged and resumed arranging the cups and saucers. Then he said, without preamble, 'Petra rang me last night.'

Ashley abandoned stacking plates and turned to stare at him. Her irritation with him fled. Maybe this was the reason behind his out-of-character cynicism about relationships. 'And?'

'And nothing.' He shrugged. 'When, or if, she comes back to Berecombe, we can talk things through then.'

'Does she want a relationship with you?'

Noah's lips compressed and he became suddenly very busy turning each cup handle to exactly ninety degrees. Ashley recognised the signs. He was hurt and didn't want to talk. 'Truth,' she demanded, resorting to the language of their childhood.

He looked up and blinked rapidly. 'Truth? Rather stupidly, I think I've fallen for her and she's proving as elusive as the sea mist. Travelling the length of the country singing. Maybe it's going to be me alone and palely loitering at home as well as you?' Then he changed the subject. 'Colour scheme will work well. Pure white with the red, white and blue bunting.'

'And I've got some silver balloons to blow up too. I'll tie them to Ruby's chair. Oh, Noah.' She went to him and put her arms around him, hating to see him in pain. 'I'm sure it will all work out and I don't mean the colour scheme.'

'And if it doesn't?'

'Then it wasn't meant to be.' She gazed into his eyes. They were troubled and stormy. 'I'm so sorry. I'm here if you want to talk. Or share a beer. Or pizza.'

'Thanks, Ash. I'll just keep busy. Don't have any problem doing that.' He sucked in a deep breath. 'Now where are these balloons you promised me?'

Ashley turned, looking for them and putting a hand to her eyes against the glittering light bouncing off the sea. Then she gasped. 'Forget the balloons. I think there's someone here to see you.'

'Hi, Ash. Noah.'

It was Petra. She was in her full Jenny WRENs gear, a slinky navy-blue RAF uniform which skimmed her curves like a second skin. With her blonde hair piled up on her head and a face full of eyeliner and scarlet lipstick, she looked stunning. Ashley felt very sorry for her cousin. He was standing, open-mouthed, holding a tray of cups.

Gently, she took it off him. 'Go and talk,' she urged. 'We can manage here. There's not much more to do. Go on.' She gave him a little push. 'You're always on at me to talk things through – well, now it's your turn.' She tried not to get her hopes up for them as they walked off towards a bench in the distance.

Chapter Seven

Gradually the trestle tables began to fill up as each guest, most carrying their own chair, arrived. The red, blue and white bunting fluttered in the sea breeze; Arthur and Zoe had tied the Union Jack, the Stars and Stripes and the green flag of Devon, with its white cross of St Petroc, onto lampposts and they too flapped against a blue sky scudding with clouds.

Victor, the last remaining GI veteran guest, smart in his blazer and cap, was helped by his family into place. Ruby and Serena, wearing pretty summer dresses, settled themselves next to him. Biddy, in an enormous straw hat, a 1940s frock and gloves, and Arthur sat opposite, with Beryl and her husband next to them and Zoe on the other side. It seemed most of Berecombe had turned out. Millie, baby Bobbie and handsome husband Jed were there, Alex Henville from The Henville Hotel and Eleri sat next to them, and the boisterous Tizzard clan a little further down. Emma Tizzard, in land-girl dungarees, sat with fiancé Ollie, her parents and younger brother, talking animatedly to Amy from the bookshop and boyfriend Patrick. Everyone was chatting happily, holding their faces up to the sun, enjoying the weather, or admiring the feast of cakes and sandwiches laid out in front of them. While the street party might be wartime in theme, there was no hint of rationing about the quantities of food.

Once the army of teapots had been filled and distributed, the WI team sat down. With the lack of traffic and everyone in their 1940s finery, it really felt like time travel. Farmer George Small lounged on his straw bales and was surrounded by a bevy of land girls. If a Spitfire had buzzed across the sky, dipping its wing in salute, Ashley wouldn't have been at all surprised. Going to the microphone Noah had rigged up to the sound system, she gestured to Zoe, who was manning it, to switch off 'In the Mood'. It should have been Noah who made the welcome speech, but he and Petra were nowhere to be seen. Someone needed to introduce the event, to present Ruby with her birthday cake and to thank Victor. And it needed to be done now before everyone was distracted by food and then wandered off with tummies full of

Spam sandwiches and jelly and ice-cream. A flash of a cream linen suit at the very edge of her vision reassured her. Eddie had made it. He waved and gave her the thumbs-up. It gave her a little courage. She had no option; she'd have to do it. Her stomach churning with nerves, she cursed her cousin, cleared her throat and began speaking.

'Boys and girls—' The microphone screeched and she jerked back. Not the best of starts. Oh God, could she do this? 'Ladies and gentlemen,' she continued a little further away from the mike. 'Visitors and residents of Berecombe and honoured guests. Welcome!' She ignored the whoop from Zoe and ploughed on. What on earth could she say? She had no idea what Noah had planned, save the playing of both national anthems. She'd just have to wing it. 'I haven't lived in Berecombe for a year yet. When I arrived, I was ill, lonely and without a job or friends. Your wonderful weather helped me heal, your warm welcome enabled me to make friends, and a very kind and patient man called Ken gave me a job.' There was more whooping, this time from the Tizzard clan.

'I've come to love the town and what it offers. Like many before me and many to come. But the most special quality Berecombe has, its strength and its uniqueness, comes from its community. This town's community is something entirely unique. It's what has seen it through difficult times. The community pulled together in the past, during World War Two, and offered the visiting GIs a much-needed home from home. More recently, the community worked together to support a local business when the opening of a big chain café threatened it, and rallied to fund-raise when the Regent Theatre roof collapsed. You came together as a community to say farewell to one of your own earlier this year. When I asked you to attend Jimmy Larcombe's funeral you came in your hundreds to honour a man who had given so much to the town.

'And now we've come together to honour others who have helped make Berecombe the special place it is. Two of them are here today. One is Victor Williamson, who, aged twenty, left his home in South Carolina and travelled to Devon to fight in a war on our behalf. Victor has loved all the commemorative events that have happened this summer so much that he's still here! This street party is to say thank you to Victor and his countrymen for the sacrifices they made. Can we please be upstanding to listen to "The Star-Spangled Banner".'

Zoe pressed play and thankfully, the US anthem began. When it finished and everyone sat down again, an impromptu round of 'For He's a Jolly Good Fellow' began, with cheers and applause. Victor beamed and his daughter dabbed her eyes.

'And now, if you can bear with me for just a minute longer, we have another guest to honour today. She's a woman who first came to Berecombe also because of World War Two. She didn't come as a soldier. Instead, she travelled as a young girl, an evacuee fleeing the Blitz in London. She lived with the Larcombe family at the grocery shop and has many fond memories of her time here during the war before she left Berecombe as a young adult. So much so, she returned to Berecombe for Jimmy Larcombe's funeral and has stayed on. One of the many things she's done whilst here is record her memories as part of the Living Memories Project which will be unveiled at the museum very soon. I urge you all to visit. This month, she celebrates a milestone birthday. Can we all sing "Happy Birthday" to Mrs Ruby Daniels, ninety-two this month!'

As a fairly riotous version of 'Happy Birthday' was sung, Biddy brought on the cake, festooned with candles. She placed it in front of a delighted-looking Ruby, who, once the singing had finished, gave a regal wave and blew them out. After the cheering, Ashley tried to get the crowd's attention but it was to no avail. She mouthed, 'What can I do?' to Zoe, who pressed play again and the national anthem rang out, shutting everyone up as they stood to attention. Not giving them time to start chatting again, Ashley then announced the street party open.

As she passed behind Ruby's chair, the woman clasped her hand. 'Thank you, dearie,' she said, tears sparkling. 'Thank you. I've had the time of my life.'

Ashley looked down at her, emotion swelling in her throat. 'Thank *you*, Ruby.' She nodded to the feast lined along the tables. Sandwiches, scones, specially made pies with the glut of local blackberries and clotted cream, of course. It was traditional fayre but all home-cooked and looked delicious. 'Enjoy.'

She flopped down in her own chair just as Tash, the manager of the estate agent's, walked past. Ashley was a little in awe of the woman, who was always rushing around in sharp suits and stilettoes and was rumoured to take no prisoners.

'That was absolutely great, Ashley.' To Ashley's shock, Tash reached in to kiss her cheek. 'I'll make sure head office get a full report of today. I know they'll think the sponsorship was worth every penny. Hopefully, now you can relax and enjoy the rest of your day.' She beamed adoringly up at an enormous man with a strong crooked nose who was standing at her side. 'May I introduce you to my fiancé, Kit?'

'Hi, Kit.' Ashley smiled at the man, who was even bigger than Eddie. She was enjoying seeing Tash's softer side; it made a change from her uber-efficient estate-agent persona. 'Nice to meet you.'

Kit grinned and Ashley saw what had attracted Tash. 'And you.' He tugged Tash to his side and dropped a kiss onto the top of her head. 'What can I say? She's only marrying me for my money, but I thought I'd take her off the streets.'

Tash tutted and elbowed him in the side. 'If only.' She turned to Ashley. 'He hasn't a bean. Ploughs it all into the animal sanctuary he runs. What did you take on last week?' she demanded.

Kit pretended to look shamefaced. 'Fifty guinea-pigs and a small herd of alpacas.'

'And they all need feeding and mucking out and it all costs money!'

He bestowed a loving smile on his fiancée. 'What can I say? I'm just a soft touch for strays and lost causes.' They were lost in one another's gaze for a moment. Then he remembered they had an audience. 'You're very welcome to visit, Ashley. We're only just out of town. Come over one day and we'll show you round. We promise we won't make you muck out any alpacas unless you really want to.'

Ashley laughed and they drifted off.

'High praise from Devon's Business Woman of the Year,' Eddie said as he passed her a cup of tea. 'And she was right. You did great, kiddo.'

Blowing her hair out of her eyes, Ashley swore

quietly. 'Wait until I get hold of Noah. He really left me in the lurch.' She gulped her tea down in one.

'Wait, you weren't supposed to do the speech?'

'No,' she replied indignantly. 'Not only did he disappear with Petra for ages, but he didn't tell me what he wanted to say. Oh!' She gasped, putting a hand to her mouth. 'I didn't thank anyone!'

'Don't worry. The prodigal has returned.' Eddie nodded to the far end of the tables where Noah was shaking hands, bestowing kisses on the women and clapping men on the back. 'I'd say, guessing from the body language, that things with Petra went well. Looks like he's doing enough thanking for the both of you.'

'I'll flaming well kill him. I stand up and make an idiot of myself and he swans in and gets all the glory.'

Eddie laughed and, pulling her to him, kissed her on the cheek. 'You did a fantastic job. If that was you on the hoof, I'd love to see you when you'd planned something. It was personal, from the heart and' – he grinned wickedly – 'short.' He waggled his eyebrows comically. 'Sandwich? I believe they're Spam and tomato.'

Ashley took one. After all the hard work of the morning, she was starving. 'Thanks.' She looked around. Everyone was chatting, drinking tea, devouring sandwiches and cake and having a great time. The sun was shining down, the bunting fluttered in the breeze and Biddy, from her place further up the table, gave her two thumbs up. A major compliment from a woman who rarely gave them. Her work was done. When Petra took her position at the microphone, blew her a kiss from scarlet lips and began to croon 'Sentimental Journey', she finally began to relax.

Chapter Eight

As the afternoon slipped into a mellow-lit evening, most people packed up their tables and chairs and left. A few hardy souls, led by George Small, had cracked open a flagon of scrumpy and an impromptu game of cricket started up on the deserted road. With people sprawled on the straw bales and the thwack of leather on willow, it couldn't have been a more English scene.

Ruby and Serena wandered to where Ashley and Eddie sat, with legs lazily stretched out, watching Sean Tizzard hit a six, luckily sending the ball over the prom and onto the beach.

Ruby slid into the chair next to Ashley's. 'Lucky that didn't land on a car,' she giggled. 'You seen what your Noah's given me?'

'No, but he said he had a surprise for you. What is it?'

'A book.' Ruby held up a thin A4 volume. 'It's got all the recordings I've done written up. Permanent record, like. Wasn't that kind of him?'

'It was. Very kind.' For this Ashley thought she could forgive Noah his earlier absence. After all, she'd encouraged him to go off and talk with Petra. It was just bad timing that his absence coincided with when he should have been making his speech. 'And what a lot of hard work,' she added. 'It must have taken him ages. What a lovely thought. You'll be able to read through at your leisure and pass it on to your family, if you want to.'

'I will. I'm ever so pleased with it. I'll treasure it.' Irritably, she addressed her daughter. 'Sit down, Serena, take the weight off. I'm not going anywhere soon.' Putting the book on the table, she turned to Ashley and took her hands. 'Biddy's just told me all this was your idea. I've had one or two surprise parties sprung on me before. Our Serena put us all up in a swanky hotel for my ninetieth. It were grand. Big white joanna in the reception, we had cocktails and an afternoon tea. Lovely. Last time we had all the family together.' A delighted smile spread on Serena's face. 'But this was just as nice.' The smile disappeared. 'This time I had all me Berecombe family with me.' She put her face up to the sunshine and drank it in. 'And it feels good to be out in the fresh air. You can't beat the salty Berecombe air. Does wonders. I always thought that. Thought that the very first time I got out of the car and walked up to Florrie's shop.'

'We drove past the old grocer's where Mum stayed during the war,' Serena interjected. 'It's a rather nice gallery now.'

Ruby snorted. 'None of that when I was here. None of those "We Saw You Comin'" shops. We had a bakery, a butcher's, a post office, a picture house. There was even a garage in the High Street, not that it did much business in the war, what with all the cars up on jacks for the duration. And in the harbour, there were so many fishing boats.'

'Well, things change, Mother,' Serena bristled, perhaps sensing her mother was becoming maudlin. 'And may I remind you my art gallery has kept us going for the past fifteen years, and in some considerable comfort, I might add.'

Not for the first time, Ashley felt a pang of sympathy for Ruby's daughter.

'I know things change. I've been on this planet long enough to realise that. What hasn't changed is community. It came together in the war, and it came together today.' The old woman's eyes glistened. 'Look at the work that's gone into today. These things don't

71

happen overnight. You need someone to get the tables organised and a team to make the food, sew the bunting and get it strung up. All sorts. It took me straight back to the street parties we had when the war ended. Mind you, there were no cars about then, so it didn't matter one jot that we used the street. We didn't have a spread like this one, but we scraped together the rations as best we could. We were just relieved to have made it through.' Her voice choked. 'Those that did, I mean.' Clearing her throat, she laughed a little. 'I remember at ours we had a Best Fancy Hat Competition. Young Clive won an onion for his.'

'Why, wasn't his hat any good?' Ashley asked.

'Get on with you, it was the First Place Prize!'

'An onion?'

'Scarcer than gold in those days, dearie. He took it home pleased as Punch.' She took Ashley's hands. 'Different world. Can you imagine a time when it was hard to get hold of something like an onion?'

'I can't.'

'Well, there was an' all. I want to thank you, Ashley, lovie. For making my return to Berecombe so special. For listening to me rambling on about all my memories. But, most of all, for making today happen. I've enjoyed every minute.'

Ashley smiled at her, tears welling. She'd miss Ruby

so much when she returned to London. 'I couldn't have done it for a more wonderful woman. I've learned so much from you, Ruby. I think we all have.' Leaning over, she hugged her gently.

'Yes, well,' Ruby said, straightening her cardigan and bobbing her hair back into place, damping down the threatening emotion. 'I'll miss you, Ashley.' She nodded to Eddie. 'And your young man. You learned any more about your grandfather, young Eddie?'

'I finally got some of his war papers through.' He glanced at Ashley. 'Only just got them in the post. Haven't had much of a chance to go through them but, from what little I've read, although he made it through, he was injured and spent some time in various hospitals after D-Day.'

'He won't be alone in that,' Ruby said crisply. 'I sometimes count my blessings to be born a woman. At least it meant I missed all that lot.'

Ashley took Eddie's hand, concerned. 'I'm so sorry. He must have been through hell.'

'Yeah, think he did. Had some injuries to the head. Not nice.'

'At least you know a little more about him though,' Ashley offered.

'There is that.'

'You've got a little bit of your grandfather to keep,

that's good,' Ruby said. 'I wish,' her voice faltered, 'I wish I had something of my Chet's to keep.' Her hand went to the locket around her neck.

Serena stood up abruptly, obviously hating seeing her mother stray into grief. 'We really need to be going.' Addressing Ashley, she added, 'Thank you for making it such a wonderful day for Mum. It's been splendid.'

Ruby let her daughter help her up. 'We'll see you at Noah's exhibition.' She chuckled. 'When all my dirty secrets are aired to the world.'

'I sincerely hope not,' Serena snapped in alarm. 'Or there will be words.'

Chapter Nine

'Well, I think it's finally ready.' Noah looked around the exhibition space in the main room of the Arts Workshop. He and Ashley had collapsed onto chairs at the end of another hectic day. 'So glad Ken let us have it here. There wouldn't have been nearly enough space for it all in the museum.'

It was the same room which had hosted Jake's paintings but it couldn't look much more different now. Gone was the echoing white space, deliberately designed to leave breathing space for Jake's spectacular portraits. In its place were carefully segregated areas, each with a bench and a multi-media screen display. They were shaped so cleverly that any sound was directed inwards. Only the people sitting on the bench would be able to hear the sound reel. Over the past few weeks Noah had worked with Ruby on what to choose for the exhibit. Between them they'd edited out the most intimate details but had included the story about Christmas, Ruby's poignant description of the GIs leaving and Jimmy's experiences at Dunkirk. Her tapes alone filled four sound booths. Even Ennis had come up trumps in the end, with stories his father had told him about life on the allotment during the Dig for Victory campaign.

Around the room, blown up to an enormous scale and printed in black and white, were Ashley's photographs. Most featured residents of the town but a few shots of Berecombe were included, too. The town hall loomed eerily in the atmospheric dusk light; the stretch of promenade glistened with reflections of mistily glowing lights in the rain puddles and a café and bookshop, stood against a darkening sunset-striped sky. In the middle of the room was a display to complement the taped recordings. A banner hung from the high ceiling, proclaiming *Berecombe Living Memories*, and Biddy's bunting added a celebratory touch.

'It looks great, Noah. You must be pleased.' Ashley regarded her cousin with affection. He looked grey with fatigue but the happiest she'd ever seen him.

'It's what I'd envisioned, more or less. I wanted to tell the story of the town through its members, to be a celebration of all that it is. I wanted those voices who don't get heard to be showcased. You know, the ordinary people who just got on with stuff. We hear about kings and queens, don't we, politicians and warmongers, but the shopkeepers and the firefighters, those toiling away in their allotments and saving lives at sea, they rarely get a chance to tell their stories. Ruby's contributions have been the icing on the very considerable cake. She's brought the war years alive in a way I'd never thought possible.' He took a breath. 'Sorry, Ash,' he apologised. 'It's the relief it's actually happened. It's making me giddy.'

'I'm not at all surprised. I'm very proud of you, coz.'

'Truth?' he asked, flicking back to their childhood phrase.

'Truth. Absolutely. I hear the Olds are coming tonight?'

He grinned. 'Ma and Pa and your two of course.'

Ashley shifted guiltily. 'I haven't seen them since I moved down here.'

'But you've rung?'

'Not as often as Mum would like.'

He waggled his eyebrows. 'You have been busy.'

'Tell me about it. And now I'm teaching two more classes on Mondays and planning more for later in the term, plus Biddy and Beryl have badgered me into leading the fund-raising campaign to improve the outside here.'

'But you're happy?'

'Couldn't be happier.'

'And it's going well with Eddie?'

'It is, although I keep reminding him, we haven't been on a proper date yet.'

'Is he going to make it back from filming to get here for the opening tonight?'

'He should do. He said they'd wrapped the first programme's filming.'

'Get you with the jargon,' he teased. 'What's the first one about?'

Ashley tugged gently on Bronte's ears as she lay curled up on her lap. 'Animals. The legend of the Hound of the Baskervilles on Dartmoor and the monkey ghost at Athelhampton amongst others. Eddie was doing a bit on the relationship between dog imagery and depression. You know, the old black dog.' She cuddled the little black dog on her knees. 'Although, my darling Bronte, I wouldn't associate you with anything other than happy things.'

'Can't wait to watch it. I'm sure they'll commission another series. I mean, look at how many myths and legends come out of the Welsh Marches.'

Ashley laughed. 'I keep reminding him about that,

too. You look happy as well. How's it going with Petra, dare I ask?'

'We, too, agreed to take it slow. Can't do anything else with her zooming around the UK on tour. She'll be back in Berecombe for good in November, so we plan on spending a lot more time together then.'

'I'm so pleased, Noah. I think you two are really suited.' She grinned. 'And, after all, we all knew she wouldn't be able to resist the famous Noah Lydden charm.' She stretched out her legs. 'And look at the time.' She lifted Bronte off her lap. 'I'd better put you in your cosy basket in the office, young lady, so you're out of everyone's way.'

'All the refreshments are sorted?'

Ashley nodded. 'Set up to be served from the staff room. And there are tables and chairs in Studio Two for people to sit and chat in a quiet space.'

'Looks like we're all set then.' He sounded nervous.

'Worried about your speech?' Ashley got up. 'It's the least you can do after ducking out of doing the one at the street party.'

He rose, too. 'I know, I know. Still want to get it right though.'

She kissed him softly on the cheek. 'You'll be fab, you always are.'

He caught her hand as she turned away. 'I won't get a

chance to say this later, so I'll say it now. I can't thank you enough for all you've done, Ash.' He gestured to the room. 'Not only this but working with Ruby, taking these marvellous photographs. I would have been swamped without you.'

She went for flippant to stop herself tearing up. 'And don't forget all that filing!'

'How could I?'

The sound of rattling china from the staff room interrupted. Biddy and her team were, once again, in charge of refreshments.

Noah pulled a face. 'Looks like it's show time. Ready?'

'As I'll ever be.'

———

Attendance at the opening night of the exhibition was by invitation only, but the room was soon crowded, with queues forming at the little booths. Ruby sat in the middle of the room feted by admirers asking her questions. She looked to be in her element although Serena hovered anxiously and batted anyone away who was too persistent.

'Hey there.' Eddie squeezed through the crowds and kissed Ashley on the cheek. 'Looks as if it's going well.'

She put an arm around his waist and hugged him to her. 'It is. The cynic in me might suggest some are here for the free wine and sandwiches, but I honestly think people are genuinely interested in the history of their town.'

'Why wouldn't they be?' He slung an arm around her shoulder. 'Why are you skulking in a corner? I've been here twenty minutes and it's taken that long to find you.'

'Hiding from Keeley Sharma.'

'The journalist from *The Berecombe News*? Why? She seems charming.'

'Charming like a steamroller.'

'What have you got against her?'

'I don't trust journalists ever since they did a number on me after my car accident. One even queried whose fault it was! They've always got an angle and it's always to the advantage of themselves and their paper.' She shrugged. 'Keeley was nice enough when we all had the meeting about Jimmy Larcombe's funeral way back in February, but she wants to do a story on me for some reason and I don't want that.' She turned to him, to enjoy the view. 'Enough of Keeley, I'd rather talk about you. How did filming go?'

'Okay, I think. Could have done without freezing my ass off on Dartmoor at 6 a.m. but Harri is a good guy, great fun. He wants us all to have dinner together soon.'

He scowled. 'Still not getting used to driving on the left though.' He shook his head. 'Your freeways are insane.'

'Aw, poor you.' She reached up and kissed him lightly on the lips. 'Wow though. Dinner with Harri Morgan and his missus Julia Cooper. Mixing with the stars! How could I refuse?' She twisted her arms around his waist and pulled him closer. 'It's good to have you home.'

'Home,' he said with relish. 'You have no idea how good that sounds.'

'I'm so pleased you made the exhibition.'

'Wouldn't have missed it for the world. The hours I've spent listening to Ruby have made me appreciate what they went through even more.'

'I'm glad we've had that time with her.'

'So am I.' He kissed her lingeringly. 'But much as I want to look around, do you think we can escape early?'

'No chance.' She pulled him in for another kiss, her insides turning molten as he nuzzled her neck. 'We have to wait for the speeches. Then maybe we can make our getaway.'

'Ashley!' a familiar voice shrilled into her ear. 'Would you like to introduce us to this man who appears to have his hands all over you?'

Ashley dropped Eddie like a stone. 'Mum! Hello. Good that you've made it.' She felt herself blush like a teenager and wondered why, even at the age of thirty, her mother could still reduce her to a fifteen-year-old.

Eddie rescued her. He held out his hand. 'Eddie McQueen. Delighted to meet you.'

Mrs Lydden pursed her lips but shook his hand. 'I'd like to say I've heard all about you but this' – she narrowed her eyes at her daughter – 'would be untrue.'

Noah came up behind and put his arm around his aunt's shoulders. 'Auntie Ann, I can see you've met Eddie. Or should I say Dr Edward McQueen.'

Ann Lydden raised an eyebrow, and she appeared slightly less frosty. 'A doctor?'

'Only the academic kind, I'm afraid.'

'Stuff and nonsense,' Noah said robustly. 'An academic doctor formerly of Harvard and Southwestern University who will soon be gracing our television screens.' He winked at Ashley.

Ann put a hand to her throat. 'Really?' she said, obviously impressed. 'And how do you know my daughter?'

Eddie gazed at Ashley, the emotion in his eyes burning into her soul. 'I am in love with your daughter, Mrs Lydden, and I hope to make a life with her.'

Ashley blushed crimson.

'In that case,' Ann replied crisply, 'you had better find me an excessively large glass of Pinot and tell me all about yourself.' She took his arm and led him off, the crowds parting and then merging again in her magisterial wake.

'God bless Auntie Ann and all who sail in her.' Noah looked at his watch. 'Yikes! Got to go. Speech time.' Kissing his cousin on the forehead, he added, 'Wish me luck, coz.'

Chapter Ten

Ashley had to hand it to him – despite his proclaimed nerves, Noah did this kind of thing with enviable ease and his trademark charm. It was a shame the same couldn't be said for the mayor, who, predictably, was over-wordy and pompous. When he'd finally finished, Ashley, spotting Keeley heading her way, ducked through the crowds, collected a sparkling water from the staff room and made her way to Studio Two. It was empty, save for Ruby sitting at a table sipping the inevitable cup of tea.

Ashley collapsed onto the chair opposite her. 'What an evening! Lovely and peaceful in here though. Are you alright, Ruby? You've been surrounded by people every time I looked your way.'

'Oh, Ashley dearie, I've had a marvellous time. I've

chatted to ever so many folk. So many questions asked and so many more memories jogged. Think I could fill a whole lot of new tapes. Did get a bit weary though, so Serena suggested I come in here for a rest.'

'Sounds like a good idea. Where is she now?'

'Noah introduced her to your ma. Last I saw they were having a good old chin-wag with your Eddie.'

'Interrogating him, more like.' Ashley laughed.

'I expect he can hold his own.' She cackled. 'And it never does harm to charm your in-laws. Oh, I've enjoyed the chats we've all been having. Shame we didn't have longer but I'm off home soon.'

'Oh, Ruby,' Ashley said, finding herself suddenly upset. 'I'm sorry, I didn't realise you were going home.'

'Not so soon really. I've been here most of the summer.'

'Can I come and visit you? In London, I mean.'

'I'd like nothing better. Shame we've got to go but our Serena's got to get back to work. Did you hear she's only gone and bought some of Jake Tremayne's paintings for her posh gallery-shop thing?'

'No.' Ashley smiled. 'No, I hadn't heard. You might get your portrait painted by him after all. I hear he's in London now.'

Ruby gave a dry chuckle. 'Think that ship has sailed. Besides, the prices he charges, I can't afford him no longer.' She reached over and patted Ashley's hand. 'I'm glad that didn't work out. He wasn't right for you. Won't be right for no one until he's sown a few wild oats, that one. Now Eddie, he's a nice young man.'

'I'm glad you approve. I'm quite fond of him myself.'

'Courting, are you?'

Ashley paused before answering. 'Much as I love that phrase, I'm not sure it describes what we're doing.'

'Dating then? Seeing one another. Going exclusive is what our Poppy would say.'

'I'll settle for going exclusive. We're getting to know one another, enjoying one another's company. Things are complicated with his son being in the States but,' Ashley paused as she realised the enormity of what she was about to say, 'I think I'd like Eddie to be the man I marry.'

'Of course you would. If there was a man made for marriage, it's him. And would you have kiddies? I can see you and him being happy with a brood.'

Ashley winced. Her mouth twisted. 'That depends on a lot of things. I'm still not sure I can have babies.'

'Oh dearie, that's sad. Children are a blessing. Even when they're hectoring you like my Serena does or getting all uppity and telling you they know best like Poppy does. Thinks she knows everything and more on top, does my grandchild.'

'I'd love a baby more than anything.' Ashley felt the familiar pain twist inside. 'But I'm not sure it'll happen. I know Eddie wants more.'

Ruby reached over again and held Ashley's hand. 'I can see babies in your future. A whole football team. And, if it don't happen, well, as I said, you have to accept the life you're given and make the best of your lot.'

'Thanks, Ruby, but I'm not sure I share your stoic acceptance.'

'Well, not much else you can do, is there? Live your best life, whatever Fate lands on your plate, otherwise you'll be a very unhappy corpse.'

Ashley eyed Ruby in alarm.

'It was something my old ma used to say. Mind you,' the old woman explained on a chuckle, 'that was usually after she'd been on the sauce.' She leaned nearer. 'And I expect that Eddie will be a good baby-maker.' Her wrinkled face twitched.

'Ruby!' Ashley exclaimed and they laughed.

She tapped a finger to her nose. 'It's those big hands he's got. Long fingers an' all. Bet your Eddie is right good at it.' Both women collapsed into hysterics.

'What am I good at?' Eddie slid into the seat next to Ashley, his face alive with mischief.

Ashley had a good idea he'd overheard and she

blushed for the second time that evening. She was amused to see Ruby's pinkened cheeks too.

He slung an arm around her shoulder and drew her in for a kiss on the cheek.

'Play your cards right and you might find out later,' she teased, still laughing.

'Sounds like I'm on a promise. Isn't that what you say over here? What do you reckon, Ruby?'

'I think, young man, you were on a promise from that day you blew into Millie's caff looking all fit and manly.' She tutted. 'It's just taken you two a deal of time to work it out.'

Eddie regarded Ashley. 'It has, hasn't it?' He kissed her again, his hand tightening around her shoulders. 'Just as well we've got the rest of our lives to work on it.'

'Well, it's lovely to see you two together. Gladdens the heart and I'm pleased as Punch it happened before I go home.'

Eddie released Ashley in shock. 'You're heading home?'

'Have to at some point, lovie. Don't want to overstay my welcome at Biddy's. You know what they say about house guests.'

'No, what?' he asked, mystified.

'They're like fish. Go off after three days – and I've been here a lot longer than that.'

Eddie roared. Clasping one of her hands, he said, 'I'm so glad I got to meet you. Can we come visit sometime?'

'Ashley here has already asked, and I've already said yes. You're both welcome any time.'

'As long as we don't stay any more than three days?' Ruby chuckled.

'Let's all meet up again in the café before you go,' Ashley suggested. 'One last pot of tea together?'

'Not to mention one of those buttery teacakes,' Ruby replied with relish. 'You're on, as my Poppy would say.'

'We'll see you then. Ah, here comes Serena to collect you.'

They all stood, and Ashley hugged Ruby. 'Give me a ring when you want to meet at Millie's. The teacakes are on me!'

Chapter Eleven

In the Arts Workshop car park Ashley settled Bronte onto the back seat of Eddie's car and then sat in the passenger seat. For a moment they didn't speak. Noah had ushered them out saying he'd take care of the rest of the evening and there was a whole army of volunteers to help him clear up. The rest of the night was theirs.

It felt curiously intimate sitting in the car next to Eddie in the dark. Ashley felt a little giddy with what she had planned for him. 'It'll be nice to see Ruby again before she goes home,' she blurted nervously.

'Yeah, it will.' Eddie sounded terse. Perhaps he was also picking up on the expectant atmosphere between them?

'I hope we'll get to say goodbye. Properly, I mean.' God, she was babbling!

'Me, too. Place won't be the same without her.'

'It won't. I know you're busy but let's try to see her before Christmas. Do you think your filming schedule would allow that?'

He twisted to face her and, taking her hand, kissed the tender spot on the inside of her wrist. It sent hot need shooting straight to her core. 'I'll make sure it does. Maybe we could combine it with a few days sightseeing and a show. Are you sure you didn't want to go out to dinner with Noah and your parents tonight?'

'I'm sure. I can't believe Noah lied so easily!'

Eddie laughed. 'It's not a complete lie. We are due to go to dinner with Harri and Julia at some point.'

'Just not tonight. It's just as well my mother is such a dreadful celebrity hound. One mention of Harri Morgan and she melted. She was a huge fan of his when he did *Who Dares Dances*.'

'I think Noah was trying to be kind. He knows it's difficult for us to carve out time together.'

Ashley giggled. 'Even so, I had no idea he could be so devious. I'll catch up with them all soon. Mum wants to do a proper Devon clotted cream tea so we're all going to Millie's. You were a hit with her, by the way.'

He grinned. 'I aim to please and besides, I liked her. So, what do you want to do tonight?'

'We could go back to mine.'

'For tea?'

'Maybe. Or maybe something else.' She watched, amused, as his mouth dropped open.

'Are you sure?'

'I've never been more sure of anything in my life. It's time, Eddie. If I don't have you, I might quite possibly combust.'

His brows shot up. 'Oh well, in that case, it would be ungentlemanly to refuse.'

'A gentleman has no place in what I've got planned for you.'

'Where is Ashley and what have you done with her?' he asked in wonder.

'I've no idea but I'm liking the new me.'

'Oh boy, so do I.'

'You'd better start the car then,' she added, primly. 'Or we won't be going anywhere.'

―――――――――

Once in the flat, she bolted the front door – she didn't want Noah crashing in later – and then settled Bronte in her basket. Eddie followed her into the bedroom and she turned. He seemed very big in this small space and it excited her. Unbuttoning his shirt with deliberate slowness, she stopped at each one and kissed his skin, delighting in his shivers of pleasure.

'What you do to me, I do to you,' he growled.

Pre-empting him, she pulled off her T-shirt and clasped him close. The sensation of skin on skin was dizzying and for a second she lost her balance. They fell onto the bed laughing. It cut through the intensity but the craving stayed urgent. Still giggling, they struggled out of the rest of their clothes.

And then Ashley froze. Flicking the duvet over herself, she hugged it to her. Desire fled in the panic of what she must look like. Why had she led him in here? Why hadn't she thought to turn off the lamp? Hesitancy engulfed her. It warred with her desire.

Eddie registered her fear. 'Let me look at you,' he said gently.

'I'm embarrassed, Eddie. They're horrible.'

'Your scars are part of you. They're part of the woman I love.' He lay back, spreading his arms. 'You got me naked on your bed and it's killing me not to have your skin on mine, but we can stay like this if you like. It'll kill me' – he shrugged – 'but we can take this at any pace that suits you. Hey, why don't I let you take the lead? I'm all yours to do with whatever you like.' He put one arm under his head, a wicked grin making his lips twitch. 'Do with me what you want.'

Ashley gulped. She wasn't sure where to start. For a second, she was content to gaze, taking in his every detail, from the broad shoulders and the bunch of his muscles to the fine blonde hair on his chest glistening in the lamp light. After a moment's hesitancy, she trailed her finger down the path to where it darkened at his navel, enjoying how his breath hitched. Her fingers tickled his long, muscular thigh and danced over his knee. She paused and traced the scar there.

'See. I have scars too,' he murmured.

Leaning over, she kissed it. 'How did you get it?'

'Skateboard. Trying to keep up with the big guys. Flipped the board one way and I went another.'

'Ouch. How old were you?' Ashley had no idea why she was asking him about boyhood accidents but postponing the inevitable was thrilling. She was enjoying this power she seemed to suddenly have over him. Her hand reached lower and caressed his foot, letting her hair fall silkily over him.

'Fifth grade.' The words were ground out.

Looking up, she saw, to her absolute delight, that he was gritting his teeth. He had beautiful feet, she decided, dazzled by love for him. Narrow with long toes and very sun-tanned. Sliding partly out of the duvet, she reached over him and trailed a path of kisses along his thigh and then along his side. Watching his face as it contorted with desire, she saw him tense as her lips kissed and then danced away again. This physical connection was exciting, as exciting as the emotions bubbling up inside. Eddie's hand fisted in the duvet, his chin jerked up and his eyes closed as he moaned. Delicately she flicked her tongue over his ribs. Her heart was racing, and her insides had dissolved; the power he'd given her was mesmerising. The world had shrunk to this quietly lit room, full of their love for one another. There was no one else filling her mind, her vision, her emotions. Still not ready for him to see her, she slid up his body, pressing her breasts against his skin, loving hearing him groan. Clicking the lamp off, everything became just about her and Eddie, the urgent whispered intimacy and the promise of what was to come. Daring to shake off the duvet, she hovered over him. In the filtered light she could see his eyes, vivid with desire. He burrowed his hands into her hair and pulled her in for a kiss.

'You're so beautiful,' he said hoarsely. 'And you're driving me wild.' He groaned again. 'Are we okay to do this?'

She misunderstood. 'Have you got protection?'

'Yeah. In my wallet but that's not what I mean. Your injuries. I don't want to hurt you, Ash. I'm a big guy.'

She ducked her head and pressed her burning cheek against his chest, amazed that she could feel embarrassed when sitting naked on top of a man. 'Yes,' she whispered. 'I asked the consultant when I asked him about riding a bike. He said it was time to... um... to use his words, "recommence all the usual activities".' She felt herself going scarlet. Eddie's chest quaked underneath her. 'Don't laugh.'

'Oh, honey, I hope you're going to ride me.'

'Stop it,' she protested, giving in to giggles. 'Isn't this supposed to be serious?' She slid off him and rolled onto her back, laughing.

She stopped laughing when he kissed her. Arching her back, she tipped her head in ecstasy. Vaguely, she was aware he'd swung his legs off the bed and was hunting through the pile of discarded clothes. Then he was back with her, warm and hard at her side. They kissed some more, their breath quickening, their hands becoming ever more urgent and demanding.

'It's about to get serious,' he panted.

Ashley came to when Bronte jumped on them and began pawing at the bed covers. She sat up blearily and shoved hair off her face. 'Oh, darling, do you want to go out?' She fumbled around trying to find her dressing gown.

Eddie gave out an exhausted moan. 'No, but I could kill for that tea I'm sure you promised me about three weeks ago.'

Ashley giggled. Wrapping her robe around her, she opened the door for Bronte and then flicked the kettle on. Yawning, she made tea, for once not bothering with loose leaf but instead just putting a couple of bags in mugs, settled Bronte back on her bed and padded into the bedroom. Eddie was just as she'd left him – on his front, one long arm dangling down the side of the bed. She paused in the doorway for a second, admiring his sexy back, her heart full of love for him. Hearing her return, he flipped over and sat up against the headboard. Scrubbing a hand over his face, he took the mug off her gratefully.

She sat at the end of the bed and surveyed him. His eyes were half-closed, he had stubble beginning and his hair was all over the place. She'd never seen him looking sexier. 'I hope I look in a better state than you,' she said, sipping her tea. 'Your heavy work schedule catching up with you?'

He smoothed a hand through his hair and flicked it back off his forehead. He gave her a wicked glance from beneath tawny eyelashes. '*You* caught up with me. I'm exhausted.'

Ashley smiled, hoping she didn't look too much like the cat who had got the cream. 'In a good way, I hope?'

'Oh kiddo, in the best way possible. Just you let me drink this tea and then we start on Act Two.'

'I believe British tea has miraculous reviving properties,' she said innocently.

'Sure does.'

Putting her mug on the bedside table, she slid back in with him. How she loved this man. His humour, his gentleness with her that had burned into a passion that had lit her soul.

He drank his tea in one and turned to her. 'Fully revived,' he said and undid the knot in her belt. She reached over to switch off the bedside lamp, but he stopped her.

'I want to see you this time, as well as feel you. Let me, Ash. Tell me if it's too much but you know you can trust me, my love.'

She lay passively while he slid her robe off and tried not to flinch as he began kissing her, his hot mouth searching downwards to her hips. His glossy hair flopped coolly onto her tummy and tickled.

'Why hello, little scar,' he whispered as he kissed it. 'I

name you,' he paused and looked up at her through his fringe, 'what shall I name this one?'

Ashley giggled. She couldn't help it. 'Doc?' she suggested. It was the first name that came to her.

'Then I name you Doc.' He kissed the hard ridge of skin again and moved to the next. 'And you I name, oh well, it's gotta be Bashful.'

Ashley giggled again and then gasped as his tongue found her. A wave of pleasure engulfed her inside and began to mount, making her dizzy but, to her frustration, he stopped.

He moved to her other hip and looked up. Through the haze of her desire, she saw his brows knit together questioningly. 'This one's got to be—'

'Sneezy?' she spluttered, at a loss.

'Okay.' He shrugged. 'Sneezy it is.' He kissed the scar. 'I name you henceforth as Sneezy. And this one's Grumpy, you're Sleepy, you're Dopey—'

Ashley saw his shoulders shake with laughter. She'd never think of the Seven Dwarfs in the same way ever again. She'd never think of Eddie in the same way again.

With no more scars left to name, that must make me Happy, was her last coherent thought.

Ashley lay spread-eagled, arms flung back. Little after-shocks of pleasure rippled through her. Gradually her brain settled back into normal, and she found the strength to roll over, resting one leg over his. She yearned to have his hands run over her body in that exciting way they had, to be surrounded by his care and love, but it would all have to wait. She didn't have the energy. She felt sappy and satiated.

'Are you okay?'

'No.' She shook her head against the soft hair on his chest. 'No.' She giggled. 'I'm not okay.' She lifted an arm up and let it fall. 'You've broken me,' she said without thinking and felt him tense.

'I haven't hurt you, have I?' he asked urgently.

'You haven't hurt me. Quite the contrary. All parts of me seem to be working perfectly well. In fact, working amazingly well. That was quite the most astonishing thing I've ever done.' She felt his chest vibrate with a laugh and loved him for his humour. 'But I need to tell you something.' She managed to sit up, catching her hair off her face.

He took a handful and let it trickle through his fingers. 'Then you'd better tell me what you have to say quick, otherwise I'm gonna be far too distracted.'

'I love you, Eddie,' she said simply and kissed him. 'I

love you with all that I have. I've never loved anyone like this.'

'I love you too, Ashley. With all my heart.' He took her face in his hands. 'And now I'm going to make love to you slowly and surely and prove it to you all over again.'

So he did.

Chapter Twelve

A shley and Eddie met up with Ruby two days later. Now it was easing into mid-September, the café wasn't too crowded, with most tourists having gone home. And, while it was good to have the town busy and thriving, it was even nicer to have it back for the locals. The café's bunting fluttered in the soft breeze which brought the salty sea air in off the beach. Gulls, having returned from their summer sojourn at sea, swooped and chattered outside, eyeing up unguarded chips and scones. One even ventured through the open doors of the café before Eleri gently shooed it out, murmuring endearments, or quite possibly enchantments, in Welsh.

It had been a little like holding court. Biddy and Beryl popped by, had a quick chat with them, clucked their approval at the sight of Ashley and Eddie holding hands and gathered Serena up to visit a new display of sea paintings being held at the gallery in Florrie's old grocer's shop. Millie, with Bobbie in her pushchair, came in, kissed Ruby, showed off the baby and then disappeared. Arthur dropped Zoe off to say farewell to Ruby and the two women swapped phone numbers, promising to stay in touch. Even the noisy Tizzard family bustled in, loudly said their farewells and rushed out again, leaving peace in their wake. It was as if the seagulls had spread the word that Ruby was going and the town was coming to say goodbye.

Victor's family wheeled him in in his chair and put him next to Ruby, saying they had to buy a few last-minute souvenirs before going off with Zoe, who claimed she knew the best shops for presents.

Ashley noticed Ruby and Victor exchange meaningful glances and wondered what it was all about.

'Well, it's lovely being back in the caff,' Ruby said. 'Pour us another cuppa, Ashley, lovie. Throat like a parrot's birdcage here. You got that recorder thing with you?' she demanded in a sudden swerve of topic.

Surprised, Ashley paused in pouring out another cup of tea. She thought they were here for a last pot of tea together, not to record more wartime memories. She shook her head. 'No. I left it at home. I can come by

Biddy's bungalow later, if you'd like, if you've got something to add? Tomorrow any good?'

'Well, ma'am, tomorrow ain't no good for me,' Victor put in. He sighed heavily. 'Gotta head home sometime and if I stay any longer, I'll be in breach of my tourist visa. And that ain't good. Never broke a rule in my life.'

'It's Victor who wants to tell you something,' Ruby insisted. 'At that tea party you held here, the one back in the summer, he started telling me about the nights the theatre used to put on for the troops, but the tape ran out or the thing stopped working. Anyways, we didn't get to finishing his bit and he's going home tomorrow.'

'I've got my phone,' Eddie put in. 'Could use that.' He looked around. 'It's quiet in here now, not much background noise apart from the gulls. What do you say, Victor? Better than nothing, I guess.'

The old man nodded. 'Yes, Eddie my boy. Ruby thinks what I got to say would be good to add to the museum's collection of living memories.'

'Maybe Noah could even add it to the exhibition?' Ruby suggested. 'I think it might be well worth a listen.'

'Sounds like it's too good to miss.' Eddie scrolled down the settings on his phone and placed it on the table nearest Victor. 'Okay, sir, when you're ready.'

Victor's voice was quiet, and they had to strain to

hear him but, as he warmed up and became more animated, the years dropped off him.

'I was a boy when I came over. Ripped from the fields of South Carolina, I'd never even been as far as New York but I loved my movies. Oh boy, did I. I seen the world through those films. Or thought I had. We came over before the others, the white guys, I mean. We built the camp at the top of the hill, set up the NAAFI, you know the stores, down on the harbour, got everything ready. White troops and the coloured boys they didn't mix, no sirree. The Snowdrops made sure of that.'

'The Snowdrops?' Ashley asked.

'Think I'm right in saying it was the slang term for the military police,' Eddie supplied. 'Is that right, sir, because of their white helmets?'

'You got that right, boy. Didn't pay to get the wrong side of a Snowdrop. The folk in Berecombe, though, they got no truck with any of that old colour bar. Never had a welcome anywhere like it, not from white folk. Sweet as pecan pie, they were. We drank in the pub, we watched films in the movie theatre, and they put on shows at the Regent Theatre for us. For *all* of us. But the whites went one night, and we went on another. Never went on the same night. No sirree.'

'That's awful,' Ashley protested.

'It *was* awful,' Ruby said. 'Everyone in the town thought so.'

Victor shrugged philosophically. 'Way it was back then.' He cackled. 'Took some time to change back home an' all. Some say it ain't much better even now. While I was billeted here, I got to know Mrs Young real well. She ran the movie theatre.'

'That was Stella's mum,' Ruby added. 'She and her husband ran it together before he buggered off with the barmaid from The Old Harbour. She had to do it all herself after that.'

'A good woman. I got mighty fond of her. Made it clear she didn't agree with no colour ban. Used to sneak me and my pal Eugene in on a whites' night and when the officers complained she stood up to them.' Victor laughed. 'Man, she got mad. She'd tell 'em to go to hell, saying it was her picture house and she'd do what she liked. Well, old Eugene wrote me when he found out I was coming back here and told me this story. I'd forgotten all about it but when he reminded me, it all came back to me. Mrs Young, as I said, didn't agree with no colour bar in her movie theatre, so there we were, all hunkered down to watch a Jimmy Cagney movie one night. It was getting on near the big push and feelings were running high amongst the men. Suppose folks needed to let off a bit of steam. Getting nervous for what was to come. No excuse for what happened though. It was all okay during the film, Mrs Young made sure of that. No one would dare backchat at her.'

'You're right there, Victor,' Ruby agreed. 'Think she was capable of winning the war all on her tod, that woman.'

'So, what happened?' Eddie asked eagerly.

'Let him speak, young Eddie.' Ruby tutted. 'The impatience of youth.'

Victor snorted. 'Bit of impatience going on the night we came out of the Jimmy Cagney movie, too. Eugene and me hung back, talked to Mrs Young a good while. She was fretting over the boy her Stella was seeing. Didn't want him going off to war and dying, see? When we got out, it was so late she followed us to lock the doors and we started walking back to camp. Could hear some kind of nonsense going on at the bottom end of town but didn't think much to it. As I say, things were getting het up. We knew our days in Berecombe were numbered and had a good idea of what we was going into. Next thing I know, a jeep pulls up next to us and two white GIs ordered us in.'

'What did you do?' Eddie asked.

'Refused!'

'Why?'

'What did I say, boy? Whites and the coloured folk,

they did not mix. We turned on our heel and walked off up the hill, but that jeep just went and followed us. Stopped and again they hollered at us to get in, said they'd drop us off at the camp. Eugene had had enough. He squared up to them. Said he ain't getting in no jeep with no white soldier. Thought it was a trick, see? Thought they'd take us somewhere and beat the crap out of us. Then I could hear runnin'. Army boots on the sidewalk. Coming at us fast. "Get in Eugene," I says. "Get in quick. Something's going on and I don't like the smell of it." The driver's pal pulled us on board and we shot off. They dropped us at the camp and that was it.' He leaned forward, his wrinkled face sombre. 'They'd saved us, see?'

'Saved you from what?' Ashley asked.

'Big fight going on at the bottom of town, in the square outside the Regent. You knows the one. Whites against blacks. They was probably all just letting off a bit of steam but thing was, the military police were doing diddly squat. The black GIs was outnumbered and they was getting a thrashing. These two white boys, they saved us from a beating.'

'Wow! Did you ever find out who they were?' Ashley asked.

'No time for niceties that night, ma'am, but we asked Mrs Young the day after. She saw the whole thing when she was locking up the movie theatre. Y'all, once I'd had a read of Eugene's letter, the memories flooded back. Funny how that works, ain't it? I can see them as clear as day. Remember them, too. Mrs Young told us they was called Glenn and Chet.'

There was a stunned pause and then Ruby said, in a strangled tone, 'Chet? My Chet?'

Victor turned to Ruby. 'Sorry, ma'am?'

'I was walking out with Chet,' Ruby exclaimed excitedly. 'We used to go to the pictures all the time, with Stella – that was Mrs Young's daughter – and my friend Iris and her beau, Glenn. Glenn was Chet's pal.'

'Well, I'll be!' Victor slapped his thigh. 'What are the chances? You picked a good 'un there, Ruby. If his senior officers found out, he'd have been thrown in the guardhouse. Two nice boys they were, same age as us, maybe younger. Real good-looking the driver was.'

Ruby took off her locket and, with arthritis-stiffened fingers undid the clasp. 'He was,' she said with emotion in her voice. 'He was a very good-looking boy. This is him. This is my Chet.' She handed it proudly to Victor who peered at the tiny black-and-white photograph.

'That's him, you say? Well, I'll be damned. Mighty fine fella. Did he make it back?'

Ruby shook her head, her lips compressed in grief. 'No, he died at Omaha.'

Victor exhaled. 'That's too bad.'

'May I have a look, Ruby?' Eddie asked. 'If you don't mind?'

'I don't mind.'

Eddie took the locket off Victor. He stared at the photograph for a long time, frozen into silence, his face paling to ashen. 'Oh my God,' he breathed out, stunned.

'What is it?' Ashley put a hand on his arm. She was dismayed to find he was shaking.

'That's my grandfather. He's not called Chet. That's Jan Kowalski. My grandfather.'

Chapter Thirteen

'What do mean, he's not called Chet? That's Chet. *My* Chet.' Ruby was furious.

'I'm sorry, Ruby. You may have known him as Chet but it's definitely my grandfather.' Eddie slid out an envelope from his jacket's inside pocket. 'The liaison at the regimental headquarters finally got back to me with more information. This was waiting for me at the flat in Exeter when I got back. This is my grandfather's photo. It's the one taken of him so that they could send it home if anything happened. I've never seen it before and neither has my mom. It was sent with a copy of his service record. This is Czcibor Janek Kowalski. Guess his Polish name was too much hard work for most, so he became known as Jan. I only ever heard him referred to as Jan.' He handed over the photograph. It was unmistakeably the same man as the one in Ruby's locket. Handsome, young, light-eyed and wearing a crew cut.

She ran a trembling finger over Chet's features in the photograph. 'My Chet?' she whispered, wonderingly. There was a pause while she gathered her emotions. 'I *knew* you reminded me of him.' She looked at Eddie. 'That very first day you came into here, into the caff, I knew! It was like seeing a ghost.' A solitary tear ran down her cheek. She was obviously trying, desperately, to process the information – and all it implied. 'But Chet died.'

'No, ma'am,' Eddie said gently. 'I'm living proof he didn't. He went back home to the States after the war, back to Rockport.'

'Where he ate lobster on the beach.' Ruby sounded confused.

'You can still do that. Rockport is famous for its lobster shack. He went back to his hometown, and in time married my grandma, had a daughter, Sofia, who went on to meet Brandon McQueen at the Catholic church, and they had me.'

'You're Catholic?' Ashley blurted out. She didn't know why it mattered except it pointed to how little they knew about each other.

He gave her a rueful glance. 'To my parents' shame,

I'm about as lapsed as you can get. But yeah, I was raised Catholic.'

'All this time I thought he was dead. He went home and made a life and he never came looking for me!' Ruby wailed.

Ashley got up and went to her, putting her arms around her.

Eddie let her sob for a few minutes, acknowledging she needed the time. 'I think I can answer that. Remember I said I was sent his war records? I've had a chance to read them more thoroughly now. Although he escaped with his life on D-Day, he was pretty badly smashed up. Broken legs and a head injury.' He glanced at Ashley. 'Maybe he didn't talk about the war not because he didn't want to but because he couldn't remember any of it. He spent some years in hospitals, including some for mental trauma back in the States.' He stretched over the table and took Ruby's hand. 'I really don't think he abandoned you.'

'He'd forgotten me,' she whispered.

'He had a brain trauma. It's possible he didn't have a choice. Or maybe, on some level, he chose to block out the war, as it was too painful?'

'And that included me and his son.' Another tear chased down Ruby's cheek, tracking through the face powder.

Ashley fished in her pocket for a tissue and handed it to her. 'Chet loved you. And you loved Chet. I would imagine things were horribly confused, people displaced all over the world in the years after the war. Injured. In hospitals.'

'But he'd know to write! He'd know to write to Florrie at the shop even if I wasn't there.'

'Maybe he did,' Ashley suggested gently.

'And maybe she and Jimmy chose not to send them on.' Ruby sat up straighter. 'Jimmy bloody Larcombe, hero of the parish, he bloomin' lied to me, didn't he? About Chet's death.'

'Maybe he did, maybe he didn't,' Eddie said. 'Maybe he genuinely thought Chet had died. There wasn't just confusion after the war, there was a lot surrounding D-Day. It was chaos. And don't forget, the landings were only the start of the campaign. The men had to continue fighting as they made their way inland.'

'Bless your heart, ma'am,' Victor piped up. 'You ain't seen nothing like it. Men lying here, there and everywhere, wounded, dying. Chaos don't cover it.'

'Or maybe Jimmy did lie but it was because he loved you so much,' Ashley said, grasping at straws, desperate to comfort the old woman. 'You said he repeated his proposal in the fifties. Or was it all about keeping your reputation safe?' She was struggling to take in the fact that the man Ruby had been describing all this time was Eddie's grandfather. 'We'll never know. But one thing's for certain, you've had the love of not just one but three men in your life. And that must be something to be grateful for.'

Ruby didn't look convinced. She addressed Eddie. 'So, Chet was your grandfather. What was his proper name again?'

'Czcibor Janek Kowalski.'

'Not easy to get the old teeth round.'

Eddie managed a grin. 'Not arguing with you there. Mom always says she was glad to take Dad's name and become a McQueen.'

Ruby nodded slowly. 'He told me his name once and I couldn't pronounce it. And I was happy to forget it as I always called him Chet, like everyone else did. How did he end up being called that?'

'I've no idea. Czcibor has the *ch* sound at the beginning. Maybe it came from there?' He took her hand again. 'Ruby, I'm so sorry he didn't come find you. As Ashley says, it was pandemonium after World War Two. Millions of people and soldiers displaced. Some personnel in Burma didn't even make it back to the UK until 1947. Without the Larcombes' help, it would have been nigh on impossible to find you, especially as you say you moved to London in 1944.'

'And they didn't tell him nothing,' Ruby said hotly. She was obviously clinging onto the idea that Chet had tried to find her and had been blocked by the Larcombes.

'Perhaps Jimmy wanted you for himself,' Ashley suggested. 'We know how much he loved you.'

'Maybe they felt it was in your best interests not to?' Eddie said. 'Oh, I don't know, Ruby,' he added, sounding frustrated. 'Maybe Chet never wrote at all? The more I think about it, the more I think the war changed him in some way. He never talked about it, not to Mom or me, never kept his medals, didn't keep in touch with old comrades as you have, Victor.'

The old man nodded in acknowledgement.

'I suspect he was so profoundly affected by what he saw and experienced,' Eddie continued, 'that he blanked off that part of his life as if it had never existed. Perhaps it was psychological, perhaps it was some physical injury. There's so much we'll never know.'

Ashley understood. It was the demarcation lines again. Whatever divided two parts of a life, whatever trauma, it was hard and unyielding. She hugged Ruby gently. 'In some ways it's like me, except on a much more intense scale. Before my accident I had a certain life. I taught, wanted to progress steadily up the career ladder...' She hesitated and glanced at Eddie. 'I was in a relationship that I hoped was going somewhere... and one second changed all that. God knows, I can't put myself on the same level as Chet but I know what it's like to not want to have anything to do with the life that's gone before, even if you could. A twist of Fate changes you so radically that you steer yourself off on a completely different path.' She squeezed the old woman's hand. 'And, for all we know, Chet was so badly affected by his time at the front that he lost or repressed part of that memory. But *you* never lost *him*. You kept him alive all those years, never more so than in your recordings. He'll be part of eternity now. People can listen and realise what a loving, kind person Chet was.' She glanced at Eddie with compassion. 'What Eddie's grandfather was like. And thanks to what we've just heard from Victor, we now know what a brave man he was, too.'

'And, whatever the truth of the situation, I'll be forever grateful as you've brought a part of my grandfather back to my family that we had no knowledge of,' Eddie added, his eyes glistening. 'Mom is going to love hearing the tapes. I'm going to have to revisit them all too. Listen to them knowing that Chet, the man you're talking about, is actually my grandfather. I can't believe they're the same man. It hasn't sunk in. I'm going to have to adjust my knowledge of Chet, knowing this. Jeez, it's a lot to process. Trust me, our family knew nothing of his life here in Devon.' He thrust his hand through his hair, making it disordered, and Ashley's heart went out to him.

'Ruby, would you mind if I ask you one more favour? Could we get together, spend some time talking this through? Maybe when we come visit you in London? I'd really appreciate that. I'd love to hear what else you remember about him. I know it's a lot for you to take in. It's been a helluva shock for me too. I'd love to revisit some of your memories knowing now that he was my grandpa.'

Ruby nodded. She dabbed her eyes and pulled in a deep breath. 'Never thought anything else would surprise me at my age, but this has.' She squeezed Ashley's hand back and managed a watery smile. 'I can do that, young Eddie. Reckon you're even more curious about him now you know he was related.'

'You bet I am. I can't tell you how much it would mean to me, Ruby. And to my family. We can't leave it here. And I'd love it if my mom and dad got over here and met you too.'

'I'd be honoured to meet them.' Ruby's eyes sparkled with emotion. 'I'd be honoured to meet Chet's daughter. Is he' – she stopped, choking back tears – 'is your grandfather still alive?'

'No, ma'am,' Eddie replied gently. 'He passed some

years back. But he had a good, full life and I can tell you all about it. I'd be happy to.'

'And he lives on in you,' the old woman said. She smiled at him. 'You're so like him. So like my dear Chet.'

Ashley spied Serena in the far distance. She was strolling along the prom talking to Victor's family. 'I think your daughter is on her way to collect you, Ruby. Your family, too, Victor. We'll talk again soon, even if it's only over the phone as you've got to return home. Or maybe you can get Poppy to set up a video chat?'

'I'd like that.' Ruby smiled tremulously. 'I haven't a clue what you're on about but no doubt my Poppy will.' She blew her nose and visibly began to pull herself together, looking frail and every inch her ninety-two years. 'Now where did I put my handbag?'

'Wait, before you go.' Eddie reached into his jacket pocket and fetched out a small box. 'I'd like you to have this.'

'Oh, our Eddie. I'm ever so flattered,' she said, almost back to her sharp self. 'But I don't think at my age a proposal is appropriate.'

'I'm afraid it's not an engagement ring,' he answered regretfully, a smile playing about his lips. He opened it and unwrapped the tissue paper from around the small metal object hanging from a chain. 'It's the only thing my grandpa kept from the war. I know, once Mom hears all about you and your relationship with Chet, that she'll agree with me. I can't think of anyone else this ought to go to. There's a chain fixed onto it so you can wear it next to your silver locket. Next to your photo of your sweetheart.' He handed it to a stunned Ruby who held the object in a shaking hand.

'Oh, Eddie.' She stared at it for a long moment, as fresh tears began to stream down her cheeks, and then hugged it to her heart. 'Is it what I think it is?'

'I can't bring him back to you, so perhaps this is the next best thing. It's my grandfather's GI dog tag. Czcibor Janek Kowalski, or as you knew him – and as I now think of him – Chet.'

Ruby sat with the dog tag in her hand, staring at it. Then she nodded, almost to herself, almost as if to say this was at an end. Drying her tears, she sucked in a deep breath. 'I've cried more over what happened all those years ago in the past few weeks than I've done in a long time. It makes me realise I've had a long life. Long and happy, or as happy as most folks. I started living when I turned up here in Berecombe when I was nothing more than a kid. I grew up quick while I was here. You know, I never told anyone about Chet's baby dying, excepting those folk there on the night.' She shuddered. 'Shame was too much. That's why I couldn't accept Jimmy's second proposal. I couldn't do it. I'd seen the disappointment in his eyes when he knew I was in the family way. He'd have liked it that the baby died, I reckon. Nothing to remind him I'd been with another chap. Would make it nice and easy for him to start afresh with me. But I couldn't do that. I mourned that baby; I'm still mourning him. I didn't want to pretend any of that hadn't happened. I wanted to remember Chet and the lovely times we'd had together. I wanted to remember his son. But once I realised Chet was never going to come for me, I suppose, in a way, I felt the same way he might have. Wanted to put what happened to me in the war behind me. Start again. Certainly as far as Jimmy Larcombe was concerned. He was all wrapped up in me and Chet and what happened here.'

As Serena came into the café, Ruby wiped her eyes and nose, unwilling to show how upset she was in front of her daughter. 'And I did. Chet went on to have his new family and so did I. War!' She snorted. 'Messed up a generation good and proper. Chet was lucky he could move on and so was I. Don't pay to play the "what if" game though.' She shot Eddie a steely look. 'Yes, maybe I could've been a GI war bride and ended up in the US. Maybe I could have been your grandma, but we'll never know so it isn't worth guessing about.'

'What do you mean, mother?' Serena asked. 'What *is* going on?'

'I'll tell you later.'

Eddie got up and went round to Ruby's side of the table. He smiled, taking her wrinkled, brown-spotted hand and kissing it. 'In some ways, I'll always think of you as my grandmother. A bonus one.'

'You're very sweet. I'm glad I returned to Berecombe and had this summer. I wouldn't have missed that for the world.' She patted her confused daughter's arm. 'And I'm glad I had Alan and my Serena, even if young Poppy is trouble. The life you lead is the one you're meant to be given, I reckon. Don't do to dwell on what might have been.'

Eddie and Serena helped her up. 'Goodbye, lovie,' she said to Ashley, hugging her.

'It's not goodbye, Ruby. Never that.'

She hugged Eddie too, holding onto him for a long time. 'Not goodbye then. Only... what do they say? *Or revere.*'

'*Au revoir*, Ruby,' he replied. 'We'll be in touch.'

Ruby took her daughter's arm and they followed Victor and his family along the prom and were swallowed up by the soft September light.

Ashley went to Eddie and wrapped her arms around him. They watched as Ruby's figure, with its upright back and stiff shoulders, disappeared. She'd never admired the old woman more.

Chapter Fourteen

E ddie left early in the morning to head back to Bristol for a production meeting. Everyone, he said, was very happy with what had been filmed so far and a new series was already being discussed.

Ashley lay in bed, drained. They hadn't slept much. They'd lain awake reading through his grandfather's war records and talking over the revelation that he and Chet were the same man. She could feel Eddie's exhausted shock and they'd made love tenderly into the night. She hadn't wanted him to leave, knowing he was still in turmoil, but it couldn't be helped. He had to go.

She got up to make tea and feed Bronte and then returned to bed to laze. Looking around the tiny bedroom, she winced. Most of her larger canvasses and painting materials were now stored at the Arts Workshop but a few paintings were still leaning perilously against the wall and taking up valuable space. The events of yesterday, and the way Eddie had taken the news and had dealt with Ruby thoughtfully and compassionately, had decided something. She wanted Eddie close to her. She accepted he would have to leave for work and maybe to visit Hal in the States, but she wanted him near to her in the precious time they would have together. If he was only with her for a few days at a time, she didn't want to waste any of that living in separate flats.

Her tiny flat was fine for just her and Bronte but she couldn't see it working long term for when Eddie came to stay. For one, there was precious little storage. She wondered what his Exeter flat was like and vaguely remembered he'd said it was one-bedroomed, so it was unlikely to be much bigger. They hadn't discussed moving in together, but Ashley couldn't see why they shouldn't. She loved the man, he loved her and, more importantly, she trusted him more than any other person she'd ever met. It had never been an option with Piers, she realised. With Eddie she knew. She just knew she wanted to be with him as much as possible. She didn't care if people said it was all moving too quickly. She knew it was right.

She headed for a shower and, once dressed and with another mug of tea and some toast, she opened up her laptop and scanned Berecombe's community pages for any properties to rent. Her brain whirred with possibilities. In a way, it made more sense for them to live in Exeter; if Eddie was commuting to Bristol, it was easier to hop off the M5 and get into the city. She wasn't sure she wanted to live in Exeter though and Eddie seemed happy to spend time in Berecombe. She could travel in to work, she supposed, but that would involve buying a car and she hadn't driven since the accident. Shuddering at the thought of getting behind the wheel, she promised herself that driving would be the next challenge to conquer.

There was nothing to rent on the Facebook pages, so she put a search in for local estate agents. Of course, having a dog complicated things. There were one or two possibles but the prices made her gasp. Just one month's rent would wipe her salary. She had no idea how much Eddie earned but assumed he had an obligation to send financial support to Bree for Hal. Maybe she'd give Tash a call? She might know someone who had a property. But first she'd need to discuss the matter with Eddie. The thought warmed her heart. At last, she was firming up plans for a future she was excited about.

Afternoon tea with her parents, Aunt Davina, Uncle Pete and Noah was a cheerfully chaotic affair. Looking around at her family, Ashley realized how lucky she was to have them, even if her mother drove her up the wall sometimes. They had decided to stay at The Henville for a few days. Her mother and aunt planned to make the most of the spa treatments and laze by the pool; the men had golf in mind.

Millie's Café was as welcoming as ever, with its pretty bunting fluttering along the ceiling. The World War Two decorations and memorabilia had been removed and replaced with a series of prints of movie stars featured in the film festival. Apart from Alec Guinness, Julie Christie and a young and handsome Tony Curtis staring down from the walls, the café seemed to have reverted to its normal self. Two tables had been put together for the group, covered by a pale blue oilskin cloth and set with pink and blue flowery china. The bi-fold doors had, once again, been pushed right back, allowing the sounds and scents of the seaside to stream in.

Eleri brought them all a fresh pot of tea. 'Now then, ladies and gents, is everything alright? Can I get you anything else? More sandwiches or another bowl of clotted cream to go with those scones? Come straight from the Smalls' farm, it has.'

Ashley spoke for the group when she said everything was delicious. 'Any news on who Millie has taken on to run the café?' she added.

Eleri flicked her long golden-brown plait back over her shoulder. 'Last I heard it was between two candidates. A woman who used to run a beach café in Cornwall, moved abroad and wants to get back in the game, and a man. He's Michelin star trained, apparently, and would probably gear the café more to a restaurant for the evenings, I'd imagine.'

'The beach café woman sounds ideal.'

'She does, I agree, but sometimes it's not just down to experience, is it? It's got to be the right person for the job, hasn't it? Mind, she's lucky to have the choice of two such good people. It's so hard finding staff at the moment and running this place isn't for the faint-hearted.' Eleri grimaced. 'As I'm finding out. It's a lifestyle.'

'Maybe they could do it together?'

'There's an idea, now. I'll mention it to Millie.' She

smiled, which had the effect of hypnotising the men. 'So, if you're sure I can't get you anything else, I'll leave you in peace,' she said and then glided back to the kitchen.

'What an arresting-looking woman.' Ann stared at the woman's retreating back.

'I'm surprised you haven't bumped into her at the hotel. She helps Alex Henville run it. I suppose she's had her hands full with the café on top as well. She's rumoured to be part mermaid apparently,' Ashley said innocently and sipped her tea.

'I can well believe that.' Her father sounded dazed.

'What nonsense,' Ann retorted. 'Put your tongue away and go back to your golf talk, Richard.' She took a tiny scone and added cream and jam and turned to her daughter. 'I have to say, your Berecombe isn't quite what I expected. I thought it would be a dead-end sort of place that had seen better days, but I'm quite impressed. With the theatre and the museum and Arts Workshop, it's all rather lively. And I'm pleased to see how much better you look, darling. It obviously suits you living here.'

'It does.'

'Now, Ashley, is it serious with this Eddie?'

'Yes, it is.'

'Good.'

'I hear he passed the test. You liked him.'

'I did.' Her mother shrugged. 'A trifle over-confident perhaps.'

'He can come over that way when you first meet him but he's really not. He's kind and considerate and incredibly thoughtful. He makes me feel good about myself. Good about the future.'

'Of course, the situation with the baby isn't ideal but I'm sure you can both work around that.'

'I'm looking forward to meeting Hal. And if... if I can't have any babies of my own, then I'll try to be the best step-mother I can be.'

'Which isn't always easy,' her mother said shrewdly.

'I know, Mum.'

'And don't write off having your own babies. It may still be possible.'

'Mum, when you got pregnant with me did you worry about having twins?'

Ann stared at her daughter. 'Where's this come from?'

'Well, Dad and Uncle Pete are twins and it's supposed to run in the family, isn't it? And I'm tall and that's supposed to increase the risk, although I'm not sure if that's an old wives' tale. And the longer I leave it before I try to conceive apparently ups the likelihood of having them. Something to do with a surge in hormones.'

'Sounds as if you've been doing your research.' Ann stirred milk into her tea thoughtfully.

'I have a bit,' Ashley admitted.

'It didn't occur to me, to be honest.' Ashley could see her mother thinking. 'Although it must have done. Yes!' she cried. 'I remember now. I talked to Davina when she became pregnant with Noah. We discussed how it would be, having two babies at once.'

'Hard work, I'd imagine.' Ashley winced.

'But a complete family all in one, I suppose, darling.'

There was a wistful note in her voice. It was unexpected; her mother was usually brisk and practical.

'Did you want more children?'

Ann's face clouded. 'I did. But I had several miscarriages after you so decided to stop with perfection.' She smiled tremulously.

'Oh, Mum, I didn't know.' Ashley put a hand on her mother's.

Ann shrugged. 'It's not something that's easily brought into conversation. People weren't as open about such things thirty years ago. I still mark each one in my own quiet way.'

'I had no idea. It's not much fun being a woman sometimes, is it?' Ashley thought of Ruby and all she'd been through – and now, it seemed, so had her own mother. She squeezed Ann's hand, thinking how strange it was that she knew so much of Ruby's life and so little about her mother's.

'It isn't on occasion. But then again, it's rather miraculous being able to grow a human being inside us, isn't it?' She popped a fragment of scone into her mouth. 'Does Eddie want more children?'

'Oh yes. I think he'd have an entire baseball team if he could.'

'And what's he going to say if you can't provide this baseball team?'

'I think he's happy to go with the flow. Accept whatever happens when it comes. And at least he has Hal. If I can't give him children, at least he has his son.'

'Sounds to me as if you need to get along to your consultant and see what he says.'

'I've an appointment next week, as it happens. Do you think I could cadge a lift back to Shropshire with you and Dad? When are you thinking of going back?'

Ann beamed. 'Oh darling, it would be so lovely to have you home for a while. We're not heading home until next week. Richard is enjoying the golf courses down here and I have to admit to appreciating the luxury at The Henville. It'll be rather a squish with you and Davina and Pete in the back of the Jag but I'm sure we'll manage. What about your work, though, and I trust you're not going to bring that mutt along with you?' She shuddered delicately.

'I've only got classes on Monday at the moment; I'm

not starting a Tuesday class until after half term, so can square it with Ken, and Biddy's offered to look after Bronte. I suspect she's at a bit of a loss now Ruby's gone home.'

'Ruby? Oh yes, that extraordinary old woman. What a character. Well, what if we delay until Tuesday and squeeze you in somehow? How will you get back though?'

'I'm a big girl, maybe I can get the train. Although I was wondering actually, if you still had Great Aunt Pat's Fiesta in the garage?'

Ann put her hand out to block the question. 'Don't go there.' She tutted. 'Your father was supposed to have sold it for her months ago.'

'Do you think he'd sell it to me?'

'Oh, Ashley, do you think you're ready to start driving again?' Ann put down her scone, aghast.

'I've got to have a go at some point. The public transport down here isn't brilliant, especially now it's on a winter timetable. A car would make life easier in so many ways.'

'But you'd be back behind the wheel.' Ann's eyes went huge with worry and fear. 'And the roads are so busy and you'd have to drive on the motorway!'

'I know. I can't say I'm feeling all that confident about it myself, but I'd like to give it a go. Maybe Dad could give me a few refresher lessons? See if I've remembered how to do it.'

'Maybe.' Ann sniffed and reached for her teacup. 'I do like this mismatched china. So pretty.' The comment quite clearly signalled an end to the conversation.

Chapter Fifteen

It was good to touch base in Ludlow. Ashley spent time with her mother and caught up with a few old friends. Her father, in the meantime, took the Fiesta to a garage to have it thoroughly serviced and gave her a few driving lessons.

The first attempt had ended in Ashley not even able to sit behind the driving wheel; she'd fled, white-faced, into the house and had stumbled upstairs to her childhood bedroom. There she'd hugged her old teddy bear and friend, Scruffy Ted, given herself a stiff talking to and had returned to the car. Her father tried a different ploy and drove them to a disused airfield. Ashley took time to sit in the passenger seat while he parked up, then swapped to the right side and managed to sit in the driver's seat, forcing herself not to look over her shoulder in case an imaginary lorry lurched into view – the one that haunted her nightmares.

'That's enough for today, I think,' Richard began to say. 'You've made great progress, but we can head home now. Your mum's doing her special cassoulet tonight.'

'No, I want to try to drive, even if it's just for five minutes.' Ashley felt cold sweat bead on her forehead and her heart hammered against her ribs; she felt sick. As she gripped the steering wheel, she could see white knuckles. 'I'm determined to do this, Dad.' She pressed start and eased the clutch out and the car inched forwards. Her breath hitched and then she forced herself to breathe normally. It was impossible to do her calming breathing techniques and drive at the same time. Having to concentrate on handling the car demanded her full attention; ironically, it made her forget her nerves and, to her delight, the skills gradually returned. The anxiety over driving was definitely worse than the reality.

After that session, they ventured onto quiet lanes and graduated onto a dual carriageway. There had been a heart-stopping moment when a lorry had overtaken and Ashley felt the panic rise, but she'd overcome it and, from then on, it had got better and better.

'You just needed to get your confidence back, love,' her father remarked, with masterly understatement.

However, even with her driving improving, she

didn't feel confident enough to drive into Birmingham to her consultant's appointment. Her parents dropped her off and then went to find lunch while they waited.

The appointment was frustrating and unsatisfactory and left Ashley feeling even less informed about whether she should have children. After a two-hour wait, her consultant, obviously rushed and under pressure, had mumbled a few meaningless phrases about the choice being hers but, if it were him, he wouldn't have children as the risks outweighed the positives. She sat glumly in the back of the car on the return journey to Ludlow, staring vacantly out of the window. Maybe Eddie's suggestion of seeking a second opinion had some merit.

When it came to her leaving, there was drama. Her mother, despite her expressed approval of Berecombe, didn't want her to leave at all, and her father was worried about her driving all the way to the south coast on her own. They'd eventually compromised: her father would drive, with Pete following on behind. They planned to stop at Gloucester services, when Ashley would take over the driving and continue the remainder of the journey on her own.

'Pete and I will have a meal,' her father said cheerfully, 'safe in the knowledge we've got you a fair way down the M5, and then head back.'

Ashley felt about seventeen again but was secretly

grateful for the arrangement; she'd been waking up in a sick panic about driving all that way. She'd loaded the car with more of her stuff, said a tearful goodbye to her mother, promising that she'd come back soon, and the convoy headed south.

It had been another tearful goodbye to her father and uncle at the services. She promised faithfully to ring them when she arrived, got into the car and set off. It was weird, very weird, driving on her own but after the first thirty minutes her grip on the steering wheel became less white-knuckled. The motorway wasn't too busy, she had tunes blasting out from the radio, and her father had reassured her the car was totally roadworthy, with four brand-new tyres, and was extremely unlikely to break down. With the promise she'd get through Bristol and then stop at Sedgemoor services to stretch her legs, she found herself relaxing just a little.

She couldn't quite believe she'd done it as she finally pulled up outside the little flat. She rang home and reported an uneventful journey, glossing over how she'd nearly ended up in the wrong lane at Bristol. Just as well the traffic was crawling along and a car let her into the right one.

She was, however, bone weary. Looking up at Noah's part of the house, she was relieved to see lights on. Perhaps he could give her a hand to unload.

Otherwise, she was leaving it until the following morning. It was misty and a September stillness hung in the air. The nights were drawing in and she was glad she'd got back before it went completely dark. Her eyes were tired enough as it was. Definitely a good plan to increase her driving stamina slowly. Through the fatigue, though, ran a warm sense of achievement. She'd done it!

To her amazement, as she put her key in the door, it swung open to reveal Eddie. Bronte ran out yapping in delight and weaved her way around her ankles.

'Hi, Ash. Hope you don't mind. Noah let me in. His father rang ahead to say look out for you. I was up there with him at the time so collected Bronte from Biddy's and prepped a meal. Hope that's okay? Not too presumptuous?'

She flung her arms around him. 'Not too presumptuous at all. There's no one I'd rather be greeted by.' They kissed lovingly, only to be interrupted by Bronte's sharp claws.

'And hello you,' Ashley said, as she scooped up the poodle. 'Have you missed me as much as I've missed you?' The dog's frantically wagging tail told her the answer.

Eddie laughed. 'I can't boast a waggy-tailed welcome but I can unload the car and bring your gear in. There's tea in the pot. Go in and grab a spot on the sofa. Car keys, please.'

She shot him a grateful look and relinquished them. Now the sharp edge of adrenaline from the journey was blurring, she was beginning to realize how mentally and physically exhausted she was. 'Have I told you you're my hero?' She kissed him again, but he pushed her off, laughing.

'Stop distracting me, or I'll never get the job done. Go inside.'

'I do like it when you show your bossy side,' she answered, yawning. Wandering into the flat, she poured a mug of tea and collapsed on the sofa, the little black dog snuggling up next to her. Closing her eyes, she listened as Eddie brought in her boxes of stuff. Then the front door slammed shut and a furry thing thumped onto her lap.

'Care to explain?' he asked, grinning.

Ashley clutched the teddy bear to her, holding him out of reach of a very interested Bronte. Stupid tears started. 'Mum must have sneaked him into the car. He's my childhood teddy,' she said, half embarrassed. She gazed at Eddie, her eyes sparkling. 'Now Berecombe really feels like home. I've got you, Bronte and Scruffy Ted!'

Chapter Sixteen

Eddie had made a chilli with rice. It was perfect, warming and requiring minimal effort to eat. Ashley was so exhausted she didn't think she'd be up to anything that needed cutting up; she could just spoon this in. By the time she'd finished and had drunk a beer, she felt a little revived. She lay back, feeling idle, not believing her luck in finding this wonderful man.

He came to lounge on the floor and held his beer bottle up in salute. 'Congratulations, kiddo. You did it. Got to take some guts to get back behind the driver's seat. Tell me all about the car.'

Ashley told him, explaining her great aunt had left it at the family house some time ago, to be sold, but her father hadn't got round to it.

'Maybe he had a plan?'

'Knowing my father, he most probably did. It's only three years old and Auntie Pat hardly put any miles on the clock. It's immaculate. I'm going to put some driving practice in and gradually increase the time I can drive before getting too frazzled. I think most of my exhaustion tonight is from the mental effort though.' She flashed him a grin. 'I can't believe I did it. I'm so proud of myself.'

'So you should be, honey. And it'll get easier from now on.'

Ashley pointed her bottle at him. 'So says the man who's still getting used to driving on the left and can't cope with roundabouts.'

'You bet. UK roundabouts are a work of the devil. Still, I've got me a chauffeur now.'

She laughed softly. 'I wouldn't go that far.' She lay back and closed her eyes again.

'You need to go rest up.'

'I do and I will in a little while.'

'I've tried my best with your bags and boxes but there's not much spare space in the bedroom. In fact, I've been thinking, it might be premature, but it feels right…'

Ashley opened her eyes. 'Yes, it's a great idea, and no, it's not too premature. It feels right to me too and, although I'll miss this little flat desperately, it's too tiny for the three of us.'

Their eyes met as they grinned soppily at one another.

'I'm so glad I met you, Ash.'

'And I can't believe I've met you, Eddie.'

'We'll talk about it tomorrow. I've got one or two ideas. Come to bed?'

She nodded and yawned. 'What time is it?'

He glanced at his watch. 'Not nine yet. You go on ahead. I'll finish up here and take Bronte out.'

Ashley levered herself up, bent to kiss him and went into the bedroom. There was hardly any room to manoeuvre but she unpacked her overnight bag and headed for the shower.

Snuggled under the duvet thirty minutes later and drifting to sleep, she heard Eddie return from walking the dog and listened to him washing up. It was cosy being swaddled under the duvet. With a giggle, she thumped the pillow to make it more comfortable. Petra would, no doubt, accuse them of fast-tracking into smug coupledom. She didn't care. It felt so absolutely right. Eddie's mobile rang loudly and she heard him curse and answer it quickly. His low tones and fragments of his end of the conversation followed.

'Hi, Mom, everything okay? Good. How's Hal?' He chuckled. 'Yeah. I miss him. I don't know. Christmas maybe? I'll have to check the filming schedule. Sure, I'd love to bring her, if that's okay with you and Pa? Who? Kevin? He's a work colleague from the university. Remember, he visited a couple of times when I was still there? No, I don't know him that well, he's more a friend of Bree's. Yeah, well that makes sense. No, I wouldn't worry, he's an okay guy. Look, it's getting late here. Ring me if you're concerned and I'll talk to Bree about it. Love you, Mom. Bye.'

Concern speared through her. Eddie had sounded worried. But sleep was beginning to blanket her, pulling her under, and so she was only vaguely aware of him slipping in beside her, gently tucking her into his side and kissing her softly goodnight before oblivion took over.

———————

She came to the next morning, a little bleary-eyed. Eddie, in his boxers, levered open the door and presented her with a mug of tea.

Ashley yawned, eased herself up and took it from him. 'Nectar!' She smiled lovingly at him through her mussed-up fringe. 'Whatever did I do to deserve you?'

Eddie preened. 'Something major, I expect.' He got back into bed. 'Bronte wanted to go out, so I made tea. Hope it's up to your high standards.'

She sipped. 'Teabag in the mug?'

'Jeez. See, I told Bronte you'd guess.'

'I'll let you off as it's such a luxury to have one brought to me in bed. Heaven, in fact.'

He gave a her a wicked grin. 'You can thank me later.'

Ashley snorted. 'You're so demanding!'

'Better get used to it, babe. It's how it's going to be from now on.'

'Think I'll cope.' Putting her mug on the bedside table, she added, 'How long can you stay?'

'A week this time.'

'Ooh, lovely.'

'We can get a few things sorted if you like. Start looking for somewhere to live. I might, if you're very lucky, take you out on a proper date.'

'Get me.' She laughed again. 'We've done this relationship all the wrong way round, haven't we? Look at us, tea in bed like an old married couple.'

'I'm not complaining.' Under the duvet, he slid a hand up her thigh and kissed her.

As she gave in to the pleasure of his body sliding over hers, she giggled, 'Neither am I. Oh Eddie, neither am I!'

The week continued in the same pattern. Eddie worked from home with Bronte a loyal companion at his side, Ashley taught her classes and firmed up another two classes for after half term – she planned to present a landscape course and one devoted to using colour, on top of the introduction to painting class she was currently doing. They shared a pub meal with Noah, who wasn't at all fazed to be playing third wheel, and, at last, had a proper date – just her and Eddie – eating seafood at Samphyre in Exeter.

Eddie had received a rough copy of the first episode of his show, *Hidden West Country: Myths and Legends*, which they'd eagerly watched together. Ashley had loved it and had been amused to see Eddie watching through his fingers.

'Aw, jeez,' he said, cringing. 'Is that how I really come across?'

She poked him in the side. 'Oh yes. The all-American boy in tight jeans. You're going to have such a fanbase, sexy man!' He'd silenced her with a kiss.

It felt, to Ashley, that life was really back on track and she'd never been happier. The cycling was making her leg muscles stronger, getting back behind the wheel had boosted her confidence to pre-accident levels, and she was getting fantastic feedback from her pupils. Everything was falling into place, and she was sure she could cope with anything life threw at them. Having the certainty of Eddie's love made all the difference.

The only nagging doubt was the outcome of the consultation. She really should have taken her mother in with her; it was always hard to absorb what was said and all too easy to think of burning questions once out of the consultation room. But in a bid to assert her independence, she'd shooed her mum away and insisted on going in alone. She regretted that now and was impatiently awaiting the letter confirming what had been said. The yearning for a baby was ever-present, worse now because she desperately wanted to give Eddie another child, a baby made from their love.

'So,' Eddie began as they lounged in the sitting room in front of the TV one evening. 'We could do with making one or two decisions. About moving in together, I mean.' He was sitting on the floor as the sofa proved too uncomfortable for both of them for any length of time. Bronte rolled over so he tickled her tummy. 'First. Where to live?'

He rested his head against her leg and she played with his hair. She loved his hair; it was thick and silky. 'Where are you going to be based?'

'At the production company in Bristol and, for this

first series, on location around the West Country.' He shrugged. 'But I only need to be in Bristol for meetings. There's talk of another series but they haven't decided on which area yet. So, depending on the outcome of that decision, I'll be filming on location there but, again, it'll be in blocks of time. It's not a nine-to-five kinda job.'

'Maybe you should suggest the Welsh Marches. There's so much history in that area and it's beautiful too. I'd forgotten just how lovely Ludlow is.'

He nuzzled her hand and kissed the palm. 'Reminds me of a conversation we had not so long ago in this very room. I'd love to see your hometown.'

'I thought you were so hot,' Ashley admitted. 'And I couldn't understand the strength of my reaction. You were a complete stranger!'

He kissed her hand again. 'I can assure you it was mutual. It was a *coup de foudre*. I've never believed in love at first sight, but I did from that moment on. I left here seeing stars and they weren't in the sky, baby.'

'Well, I'm very glad to hear it,' she said, primly. 'You had much the same effect on me.'

He laughed. 'Say you want to get laid again.'

She leaned down and whispered, 'I want to get laid, preferably by you.'

Eddie roared, jumped up and for the next few minutes there was no talk of housing. Eventually, he released her. 'It's the accent. Even though I've been over here a while now and the novelty of the cut-glass English voice has gone, it still kills me to hear you say that.'

She rested her head on his chest, putting a hand on his heart to feel it race. 'You're easily pleased. I could develop a whole repertoire of dirty talk if it helps.' She felt his reaction as he laughed again.

'I so want to gather you up and take you to bed right now but—'

'But?'

'We've got things to decide.'

She pushed herself off him and, flicking her hair back, grinned. 'The anticipation will make it all the sweeter.' Affecting received pronunciation, she added, 'But I really want to get laid.'

He groaned. 'You're not making this easy. Come here.'

Things were getting heated, with all thoughts of a discussion about housing forgotten, when Eddie's mobile rang. Cutting off a curse and shooting Ashley a regretful glance, he said, 'I have to answer this. It'll be Mom.'

'No problem.' She blew him a kiss. 'I'll be waiting in the bedroom.'

As she tidied the room, closed the curtains and put on the bedside lamps in an attempt to make the cramped room even vaguely seductive, she tried not to listen as the phone conversation got increasingly agitated. They really needed to move out of here; there was nowhere to give one another space or privacy. As she came out of the bathroom, she heard Eddie shout and then there was an ominous silence. Rushing into the sitting room, she was faced with him sitting on the edge of the sofa, head in hands, his shoulders sunk in despair.

'Eddie?' He looked up and she was shocked to see he was crying. 'Oh my darling, what's wrong? Is it your mother? Is she ill?'

He shook his head. 'She's okay, thank God. It's Bree.'

'Bree?' Ashley put a hand to her mouth. 'Oh no. The baby?'

'Yes, it's Hal, but it's not what you think.' He scrubbed shaking hands over his eyes and through his hair, taking a deep breath. 'Hal is fine.' His voice broke. 'He's flourishing and healthy, but Bree has just told my mother that he isn't mine. Oh, Ash, Hal isn't my son!'

Chapter Seventeen

'Hal isn't yours? I don't understand.' Ashley collapsed on the sofa next to him.

'You don't understand? Try being me,' he answered bitterly.

She reached for him, but he shifted from her, hiding his face in his hands again. She sat in silence for a moment feeling useless, not knowing what to do or how to reach out and comfort him. She sensed him shrinking away from her. 'I don't know what to say, Eddie. What happened? How did your mother find out?' There were so many questions. She waited until his shoulders stopped heaving. It was worse than horrible watching this man she loved so much in pain.

Eventually he blew out a shuddering breath. 'There's been this guy, Kevin Metz,' he began in a low voice, not meeting her eyes, his hands dangling between his knees. 'He's been hanging around a lot, dropping in to see Mom and Pa, cosying up to Bree and,' he paused to gain control again, 'Hal.'

'But who is he?'

'I know him, he lectured at the university for a while. He's okay.' Eddie shrugged. 'He was always more of a friend of Bree's than mine.' He snorted and added, caustically, 'And now we can see how much of a friend he was. Bree's been staying with Mom, as you know. She had a hard time with the birth and didn't want to stay in Boston on her own, so moved in for a while. Mom didn't mind, she loves babies and was happy to help.' His voice faltered. 'She wanted to do all she could to help out with her first grandchild, especially as I wasn't there.' There was a pause. Eddie bit his lip, fighting for control.

'And?' Ashley prompted gently when he was ready to speak.

'He'd been calling a couple of times a week. It started when I was there and in my gut I knew there was something off-key about it all.' He rubbed a hand over his face. 'But I let it go. Suppose I assumed he was Bree's next target.'

She remembered his strained response when she'd asked if leaving the baby was hard. She'd put it down to jetlag at the time.

'Bree explained to my parents that he was a mutual friend although that was a lie. As I said, I hardly knew the guy. Then he started visiting every day, sometimes twice a day.' His voice trembled. 'Played with the baby a lot, bought presents, took pictures of them all together. It made Mom uneasy. She got suspicious. The baby looks a lot like Bree, long and thin and dark-haired. But Kevin is six two with jet-black hair so Hal looks a lot like him, too.'

'But that doesn't mean anything,' Ashley said, flailing for a response. 'Babies can look like their grandparents, or an aunt or uncle. To be fair, when they're very young it's hard to see who they resemble.'

'Yeah, that's what I kept telling myself. But Mom interrupted Bree and Kevin having a conversation. She overheard them arguing and Kevin claimed the baby was his.' He glanced at her, finally meeting her eyes. 'He was most insistent. Mom took one look at Hal in his arms, looked at him, remembered the baby allegedly arrived early and put it all together.'

Ashley gasped. 'What did she do?'

Eddie gave a sardonic laugh. 'You don't know my mom. She's a momma bear. Will do anything to protect her cub. She bided her time, got Bree on her own, got her nice and relaxed and then went on the attack. Got Bree to confess.'

GEORGIA HILL

'Oh my God,' Ashley said slowly. 'But I still don't understand. Why would Bree do this? Play such a cruel and dangerous trick? I mean, it could have gone on for years. Think how dreadful it would be for Hal to discover who his true father was when he was older.'

'It's dreadful now too,' Eddie said on a choked sob.

'It is. I'm so sorry, Eddie, I didn't mean to disparage your pain.' She floundered. 'I just don't know what to say.'

'Do any of us?' He lay back against the sofa looking wretched. 'For a long time, for too long a time,' he said softly, 'I thought Bree was unlike anyone else I knew. Intensely intelligent, could cut through any argument like a sword, astonishingly beautiful. The most charismatic person in any room.'

Ashley winced.

'Then I began to see her other side. Her vindictiveness, her game-playing, how she did things just because she could rather than it being right or wrong.' Bronte jumped up onto his lap, sensing his despair, and he scratched at her woolly ears. 'She'd get bored and would provoke someone just to get a reaction. Like a kid pulling wings off bees. Always restless, always chasing the drama, the danger.'

Ashley wanted to say he was well out of having any contact with her – she sounded vile – but kept silent. She no longer knew what the appropriate or comforting thing was to say.

'Kevin is an okay guy but he's a lot younger, and from what I've heard hasn't got much in the way of ambition. Bree's parents are uber-conservative. They'd just about accept me as the father but wouldn't tolerate the idea of Kevin.' He gave a hard laugh. 'They couldn't introduce him at the country club.'

'And there's the money, of course.'

'Money?' Eddie looked at her blankly.

'If Kevin hasn't got much in the way of employment, he won't be able to provide for the baby and, unless Br—' She broke off, unable to say the woman's name. 'Unless she has cast-iron childcare, she's going to have to think about the hours she puts in. You were her meal ticket.'

He looked down. 'Yeah. Guess I was.'

'Is it absolutely certain that Kevin is the father?'

'Well, a DNA test will prove it. I've insisted that happens. Bree told Mom they'd been seeing each other for a few months off and on and they'd slept together just before I got back for Christmas.'

'I remember you saying you used protection.'

'We used a condom. Bree told me afterwards she'd found a hole in it.'

'How convenient.' Ashley couldn't prevent the bitterness from stinging her words.

He gave an enormous sigh. 'Looking back, it all seems so obvious but I guess I was so carried along by the thought of having a kid.'

'Having children is important to you.' Ashley felt a ball of dread lodge in her stomach.

'It is, but not to the exclusion of reason. I'm supposed to be a clever man, Ash. How could I have been taken for a ride like this?'

'Maybe Bree's cleverer. She's certainly cunning and I would go as far as to call her evil if it's true that she knew Hal was never your son.' Ashley glanced at Bronte snuggled up in Eddie's lap and a horrific thought crept into her mind. Surely not? Surely no woman could be that despicable? Not even Bree could stoop so low... 'Eddie,' she began slowly, 'you said you gave your dog to Bree to look after? Because you couldn't bring him over here.'

'Yeah. I did.' He laughed mirthlessly. 'Thought I could trust her with Bowie.' He stared at her and distress shot across his face as the same thought Ashley harboured occurred to him. His face paled. 'Oh God, Ash, you don't think—?'

'Maybe not,' she backtracked hastily. 'You said Bowie was old and unwell.'

'But healthy enough when I said goodbye to him.' He thrust wild hands through his hair. 'I never guessed.

Even knowing how Bree could be, what she could do, I never guessed *that* of her.'

Tears began to course down his cheeks and he pressed his hands to his eyes so hard, the fingers turned white. 'I'll never forgive her. For that, for what she's done to my mom, and for Hal. I'll never ever forgive her.'

Ashley pulled him to her and he laid his head on her shoulder until the sobs subsided. She hated the violence Bree had put into his voice. She'd never forgive the woman either. It had been the most wicked of betrayals. She cursed silently and wished terrible things upon Bree for the harm she'd done to this kind, loving man who deserved none of this.

They sat there for a long time, growing cold and stiff, then Eddie began to talk, quietly at first and almost to himself.

'I feel so taken advantage of, so betrayed. Violated. I feel so *stupid*. How could I not have seen through her? It's as if where I once had a clear path in front, a clear route in life, now there's nothing there. It's as if my whole worldview has distorted.'

Ashley hated his despair but understood it. She'd fought hard to put aside her suspicion and jealousy over the baby and, just as she was beginning to accept the situation, it had been turned on its head. Now that part of her life was gone, she wasn't sure what sort of Eddie, what sort of relationship would emerge. Almost from the moment they'd met, Bree and the baby had been tagging along with them. 'You have me.' She tightened her hold on him.

'You wanna be with someone so stupid?'

'You're not stupid. Far from it. Maybe your fault is you see the good in everyone. Maybe you're too trusting, and I refuse to see that as a fault.'

There was a tiny part of his voice that felt cold. As if he was inching away from her. Or was it her shrinking from him? What would the future hold for them now? If she couldn't give Eddie a child, would she lose him? Or would he stay with her but become resentful and sour? Would he cast envying glances at families around them, knowing theirs would be incomplete?

'Will I be able to trust anyone ever again?'

'You can trust me.' Ashley tried for reassuring but, even to her, it sounded hollow. For months she'd struggled with the complication that was Bree and Hal and wished they weren't part of her and Eddie. Now that had changed, in their place was a morass of prickly uncertainty.

He sat up, away from her. 'God, listen to me.' He scrubbed a hand over his grief-ravaged face. 'One whole heap of self-pity.' He caught her hand. 'Let's make sure this doesn't change us, Ash. I know everything's shot and I need time to process it all, but promise me it won't affect us.'

'I promise.' The words floated out into the tiny room, but she sensed them dissipate into nothingness.

They went to bed. Eddie curled up on his side in a foetal position, facing away from her. Ashley pressed against him, trying to will some comfort through the skin-on-skin contact.

In the early hours she was woken by him weeping quietly. She put an arm under his head and the other around his waist and pulled him tight into her. They fell back to sleep but in the morning he'd gone.

Chapter Eighteen

E ddie left a note saying he had to go to Bristol for a few days and then might have to be away on location. When he was back, he'd go to his flat in Exeter. He needed some space, he claimed. Ashley understood the need to lick wounds in private but was still hurt that he'd locked her out when he was in pain.

On the way into work, she picked up the local paper and perched on a bench on the seafront to flick through it. Most of it was the usual stuff about the football team doing well, a new boutique bed and breakfast opening, some fuss about a planning application. Then Ashley turned a page and came face to face with a photograph of herself. It was the one which the Ludlow paper had used in the coverage of the accident, the one from her old school's prospectus. The headline screamed at her:

Ashley Rebuilds After Life-Changing Accident!

Today's local personality in focus, Ashley Lydden, came to Berecombe having suffered a car accident in her native Shropshire. Ashley, despite suffering life-changing injuries which mean she walks with the aid of a stick, soon involved herself in our little community. She organised a media campaign to attract mourners to much-loved local resident James Larcombe's funeral, even appearing on television to further her cause. Her photographs of the town played a big part in the recent Living Memories Exhibition, which of course was put together by her cousin, Noah Lydden, and she featured prominently in a stunning portrait in up-and-coming artist Jake Tremayne's debut show at the Arts Workshop. Controversy seems to follow her around, however, as Jake claimed Ashley was his muse and refused to sell his portrait of her. Ashley has continued to break hearts, as she was most recently seen getting up close and personal with television hunk Eddie McQueen. Now a stalwart of the Berecombe social scene, she pops up whenever there is a party and is always on hand to spearhead a fund-raising campaign. Whatever would we do without her!

Ashley's chest heaved and she shrivelled inside at the implication that she was a publicity hound out for whatever got her in the spotlight, the suggestion that her photographs were part of the exhibition because of Noah and not on merit, and the insulting insinuation that she was a player. Tears pricked. It was more than that though. She was right back in the aftermath of the accident, with her every move and motive examined by the local press. It had even been suggested by many in the community, at the time, that the accident wasn't entirely the fault of the lorry driver who crashed into her. Now she felt newly raw and exposed, all her carefully constructed shiny new confidence leaching away. She'd told a few people in Berecombe about the accident but only a few, and she'd *chosen* those confidantes. It had been in her power who to tell because it was nobody else's business; no one else had a right to know. Bloody Keeley Sharma. She'd batted off Keeley's probing questions and hints that she wanted a story about her several times – at the meeting to plan Jimmy Larcombe's funeral, at Jake Tremayne's exhibition. The woman seemed obsessed with thinking there was something special about Ashley Lydden, had been refused her story so had written this. For most, it would be considered a harmless piece of gossip, but for her it was devastating.

Ashley looked about her. Dog walkers marched along

the prom on the way to the beach, one or two tourists were out for an early morning stroll, and the postman strode by with his trolley, a handful of letters in his hand. The sun shone with a hard early-morning light, the sea murmured against the sand, a toddler squealed in excitement as his mother held him above the water and dipped his toes. It was a perfectly normal Berecombe day.

Eight months ago, she'd sat on this very bench and dropped her painting materials all over the concrete in shock at the sound of two cars crashing behind her, the splintering metal spinning her into a post-accident panic. Since then, she'd conquered so much. Made friends, created a home, become part of the community, found a job she loved and met the man she planned to be with for the rest of her life. Now, it felt as though all was disintegrating before her eyes. Her carefully constructed new life, if it had not crumbled, was facing a seismic challenge. How could she stay in Berecombe and face them all when people might read Keeley's words and think that she was an attention-seeking tart?

_____

She went through Monday's art class on autopilot. Her carefully prepared lesson on perspective and scale was delivered robotically and even Zoe popping in to say goodbye before she left for university didn't penetrate. Half term was coming up and she'd never been so glad of an impending break.

Later in the week she spoke to Eddie on the phone, but he was guarded and monotone and the conversation was deeply unsatisfactory. It might only be imagination, but he sounded relieved to be away from Berecombe – and her. Harri and Julia, Eddie's co-presenters and now friends, had just announced their pregnancy. Ashley could feel Eddie's conflicted emotions humming down the line and understood; how could she not? When he told her quietly the result of the DNA test, that he was definitely not Hal's father, his despair was palpable, but she could find nothing within her to alleviate his pain.

Ashley sobbed herself to sleep that night, taking a confused Bronte into the bed with her. Eddie was being remote and distant and, far worse, didn't want her around when he was at his lowest. His lack of need of her only made her feel even more worthless. She craved his nearness to comfort him but how she could do it? How could she comfort a man who desperately wanted children and who had just been deceived in such a wickedly cruel way? Petra had been right – Bree had used Eddie, but it was worse than any of them could have imagined.

The letter from her consultant, when it arrived unusually early the following morning, was unexpected, as with everything going on with the article and Eddie's news, she'd forgotten about the formal write-up that followed a consultation. Going through the motions, she opened the envelope and scanned the contents.

It stated quite clearly she should under no circumstances become pregnant and bear a child as her physical injuries made it extremely unlikely she would carry a baby full term and the incidence of twins in her family history complicated matters further. To attempt to carry a baby would, in the doctor's opinion, cause great risk to her and any child. He'd added that she was welcome to seek further advice but his opinion would stand.

Ashley collapsed onto the sofa. Blackness obliterated everything. Bronte's need for a walk was forgotten, planning for the next half term's lessons seemed beyond trivial. Even her concern for Eddie moved to the periphery. Her eyes blurred with tears and an agony so visceral consumed her, she thought she would collapse. She clutched at her stomach, with its empty, useless womb, and rocked back and forwards, keening an animalistic noise that was pure pain as the grief hit her like a sledgehammer. Bronte, frightened, ran into the bedroom. Ashley thought she'd never recover, never be able to function in any normal human way again. She hid her face in a cushion, unable to comprehend anything but her own anguish.

She stayed like that for a long time, barely moving, hardly breathing. Eventually she became aware of a furry body wriggling under her arms and licking her face with an insistent, warm tongue. It was the dog. She gathered her up and held the vital little body, craving comfort.

Then a new grief attacked. Eddie had just been told the son he'd thought was his was someone else's. And now she knew for certain she could never give him the children he so desperately wanted. She just made it to the bathroom in time to throw up. Leaning her clammy forehead against the white tiles, a cold rationality gradually seeped through.

She was no use to Berecombe, she was no use to Eddie. He clearly didn't want her around to help him through this dark time. He wanted children and she couldn't give him any. What possible future could their relationship have? It would hang over them every time they walked past a pushchair containing a gurgling infant. They'd have to face it every time friends announced a pregnancy. It would eat into the love they had for one another. He deserved better. He deserved a woman who could give him what he wanted. And it wasn't her.

Mechanically, she struggled to her feet, brushed her teeth and put a few toiletries into a wash bag. Shoving a few clothes into a holdall, she went through to the sitting room to put Bronte's bowl and bag of food into a plastic carrier. She could buy anything else she needed.

Once she'd packed the car, she scribbled a hasty note to Noah, wrapped it around the key to her flat and posted it through his letter box. Getting back in the car, she secured Bronte onto the dog's special seatbelt and headed north. She wasn't even anxious about facing the motorway; she just craved escape.

———————————

When Noah let himself into his flat late that evening, he missed the scrap of paper lying on the mat. It was only when he was on his way out the following lunchtime that he trod on it, hearing it crackle under his foot. He picked it up and his eyes widened. Clicking on his mobile, he punched in Eddie's number.

Chapter Nineteen

Through the mire of her pain came frustration. The traffic was terrible. It had taken her an hour to get to Taunton and, even now, she was stuck in an interminable queue to get onto the M5. As she inched forward, Bronte gave a whine of impatience.

'It's alright, darling. Once we're on the motorway, we'll stop at the first services and you can have a run around and a drink.' Risking a glance over her shoulder she saw the dog was looking grumpy and bored. 'I'm sorry I've forgotten your toy too, but I promise you as soon as we get to Ludlow, I'll hit the biggest Pets At Home I can find and buy you all the squeaky balls they have.'

As she hit the traffic lights that controlled the roundabout which led to the motorway, doubts hit.

Ludlow. Home. Or was it? With a pang she realised in her haste to get away, she'd left Scruffy Ted on the bed. She bit down on tears, refusing to cry over a teddy bear. Thoughts chased themselves in an unending, illogical loop. Maybe Noah would pack up the rest of her belongings and have them sent on? Or perhaps he could bring them up at Christmas? Christmas with her parents. That was always fun. She glanced at Bronte again. Her mother would be apoplectic that she'd brought the dog. But she'd have to put up with it. Once the compensation money from the accident came through – the legal wrangling seemed to be taking forever – she'd find a flat and move out. Her mother would just have to lump it until then. And Bronte didn't make much mess – a splash of water around her bowl, a missed speck of kibble. Had she packed the dog's blanket? She'd ring Noah when she got home and sort it. Pay to get it all couriered. The worries nagged around and around, giving her a headache. But it was best to concentrate on practicalities. Far better. 'Don't think about Eddie,' she murmured.

The queue in front inched forward and then stopped again. Ashley thumped the steering wheel. All she wanted to do was escape. Why was it proving so impossible? She needed to get away from everything that was causing her pain.

Run away. That's what she was doing. Cut and run. It was the best way.

Run away. The words hung thickly in the air. Noah's accusation came back to her. That she always ran away from her problems. That she always refused to stay and seek out a compromise, a way forward. But surely even he would see she had no alternative? Not this time.

The traffic moved again. She was in the middle lane. It was the one to take her onto the motorway and begin the long journey home.

Except it wasn't home.

The image of her little overcrowded flat appeared. The mug that Noah had bought her, with its seaside-y blue and white stripes. The squashy sofa that always threw its occupants into the middle. Scruffy Ted sitting on her pillow. She thought of her students sitting at their easels, eagerly trying the cross-hatching technique she'd taught that week, the friendly banter at coffee time. Then she thought of Ken and how disappointed he'd be in her when she rang to explain she was no longer able to teach the classes. She pictured Biddy and Beryl's faces when she didn't turn up for the tea and scones meeting at Millie's. They were supposed to plan the next fund-raising appeal for proper security lighting for the Arts Workshop car park. They'd feel horribly let down. So would Petra when she returned to Berecombe after her tour to find her friend had disappeared.

An image of Ruby flooded her vision, in one of her pastel twinsets, sipping tea and sharing her stories. She'd fled in much the same way but, being pregnant and alone in a world still at war, hadn't she the greater need? If Ruby had even the slightest suspicion that Chet was still alive, nothing on earth would have stopped her getting on a boat and sailing to the US to seek out the boy from Rockport. Ruby faced things head on. But Ruby also found happiness in a compromise. She hadn't had the life she dreamed of but had forged a new one with her Alan and baby Serena.

The lights turned green, but nothing moved. There was a queue ahead, blocking the roundabout. A gap appeared. Someone tooted impatiently behind her. She slipped the clutch, nearly stalled, then moved forward, following the lane marked *M5 North*. The traffic ground to a halt at yet more lights on the roundabout. She blew out a frustrated breath. Would she ever get out of this traffic jam? If she stayed in this lane, she could either turn off left onto the motorway slip road or stay on the roundabout and go all the way round again. Double back and head to Berecombe.

But could she go back and face everyone? Could she go back and face Eddie? Irritated by her agony of indecision, she flicked the left indicator to turn onto the motorway and then heard Ruby's voice in her head saying quite clearly, 'What do you think you're doing? Go back and face the man. He deserves an explanation. Get yourself back home, girl.'

Home. But where *was* home? In Ludlow with her parents, or in Berecombe? Oh God, what should she do? If she ran away now, all the progress she'd made in the last few months would amount to nothing. She'd grown bigger as a person; she knew facing up to her problems was the right thing to do. It was what Ruby would have done. A longing for the old woman's company overcame her. Mad as it was, she needed to share a pot of tea and hear some wise advice.

At last, the traffic moved and she found herself surrounded by cars speeding past her. It took less time to get to Bristol than it had to get onto the motorway in the first place. Ashley had little sense of how she'd got there, distracted by her muddled thinking. She'd stuck doggedly to the nearside lane, following a truck carrying a load of logs. And then, at the bewildering junction for South Wales and London, Fate took a hand. Without indicating, the log truck took a lane sweeping off to the left and Ashley unthinkingly followed in its wake. She only realised her mistake when it became clear she was on the M4 slip road heading east and to London.

London or Ludlow? Ruby or her parents? The motorway was giving her a second chance to get back on route. But she didn't know what to do! Her hand hovered over the indicator, clicked right to rejoin the M5 – and then she changed her mind. To a cacophony of blasts from irate drivers behind her, she swerved the car back onto the M4. Brakes squealed behind. Every nerve in her body flinched, expecting the crunch and thud of metal as someone ran into the back of her. But it didn't happen. By some miracle she'd sneaked into a gap in the traffic. Not Ludlow. Not Berecombe. Finally decided about where she was going, she put her foot down and headed east.

Chapter Twenty

S he stopped at the first services she came to. Bronte stretched her legs and had a wee; Ashley grabbed a coffee and checked Ruby's address and the route on her phone. Irritated, she discovered that, had she decided to go straight to London, she needn't have used the M5 at all.

'Too late now, Bronte,' she murmured to the dog as she rejoined the motorway. 'Looks like we're visiting Blackheath. Let's hope Ruby's in.' With more than a few qualms about her ability to drive through London, she figured there was only one way to find out. 'Dad would be proud of me,' she said to the dog, who was now asleep and oblivious. 'Look how far my driving confidence has come.' Determinedly ignoring her stomach, which was hollow with fear, she concentrated on the road.

———

Unable to find a parking spot when she finally arrived, Ashley abandoned the car on the drive of the pollution-stained four-storey house. It had begun to drizzle and icy water dripped down the back of her shirt from a London plane tree above. She was grateful; it woke her up. After hours of negotiating heavy traffic, with a white-knuckled grip on the steering wheel, she'd found herself in a flat open area which could only be Blackheath Common. Swooping down the village-y main street, she'd turned off into a narrow road lined with tall Victorian houses. She'd now strayed into a surreal, light-headed state that was outside exhaustion. Following the sign which directed her to the Garden Flat, she prayed fervently that Ruby would be in. She hadn't thought beyond this point. She'd passed a hotel on the common, but it was unlikely to take dogs. As she sagged against the door and knocked, a security light came on; the day was fading fast. 'It's me, Ruby.'

'Ashley?' Ruby's voice sounded shrilly as she peered through the letter box. 'Is that you?' The door opened. 'Oh, my goodness. What are you doing here? Whyever didn't you let me know you was coming? Come in, come in, out of this weather. Ooh, hello; it's Bronte too. Do you want to go out in the garden, little one?'

Ashley followed Ruby along a narrow hallway and into a large sitting room. The old woman opened French doors which overlooked a walled garden. 'Out you go,' she said to the dog. 'Have a wee-wee while I put the kettle on. Don't worry, you can't get lost.' She turned to Ashley and stared at her with shrewd eyes. 'Summat's up. Sit yourself down, you look fair to drop. I'll make the tea and get you a bite to eat.'

———————

Having drunk her first mug of tea and eaten a cheese sandwich, Ashley felt marginally better. She lolled, boneless with fatigue, on Ruby's sofa, not believing she was here. She'd driven all this way, navigated the horrors of the South Circular and found Ruby's home.

Ruby sat opposite, in a high-backed chair, her hands primly folded in her lap, waiting. 'It's lovely to see you again, child. To what do I owe the pleasure?' She pulled a face. 'But pleasure's not what this is all about, is it?'

Once Ashley began talking, she found she couldn't stop. All the pain about Bree, the baby and Eddie spilled out. Bronte crept onto the sofa and cuddled up to her and she stroked the woolly fur. With the autumnal darkness kept at bay by lamplight, it felt almost like therapy. She told Ruby how happy Eddie had made her, how much she loved him, how she'd once hoped they could make a life together. She explained the newspaper article and how she felt betrayed by Keeley. She told her about Hal not being Eddie's son and how devastated he was. And then she paraphrased the consultant's letter. That it was very unlikely she would ever have babies and give Eddie the children he so desperately wanted. That *she* so desperately wanted.

When she'd finally finished, Ruby said nothing. Instead, she made a fresh pot of tea and refilled Ashley's mug. It was now completely dark outside, or the neon-tinted grey that passes for dark in a big city. Ruby pulled the curtains to and shut the drizzly gloom out. 'You'll be staying the night, I expect? Serena and Poppy are out tonight. It'll be good to have some company. Can't offer you anything but that old settee but it's comfy enough. I can make it up for you after we've had our tea. Nothing grand, mind. Just a shepherd's pie. Nice with a few peas and a spot of good gravy.' She settled eventually back on the upright chair.

'I'm sorry I've gone on,' Ashley said, as she sipped tea. A distant wail of a siren could be heard, and she was glad she could stay. The thought of battling another long journey today made her shudder.

'Get on with you. You've had to listen to me go on enough this past year. Do you want to hear my fourpennyworth or was letting it all out enough?'

Ashley managed a smile. 'Any advice would be welcomed. After finding myself at a crossroads earlier in the year, I think I'm at another.'

'Well, let's see. Crossroads are good. Gives you time to stop and take stock. Decide on a direction. You were off to Shropshire, is it? Why? What's in Shropshire?'

'My parents.'

'Do you think moving back in with them is a good idea?'

'No – I...' Ashley let the sentence hang.

'So why were you off there?'

Embarrassed, Ashley concentrated on tugging gently on Bronte's ears. The dog was snoring contentedly. Maybe she should come back as a dog in the next life? They didn't seem to have any of these problems. 'Noah always says I make snap decisions to avoid dealing with the problem in hand and cut and run back home.'

'Home's a wonderful place to run to,' Ruby said softly. 'As long as you know where home truly is.'

'And that's my problem!' Ashley cried, sitting up.

Bronte started and growled. 'I don't know where my home is anymore.'

'I think you do, dearie. Deep in your heart I think you know that Berecombe is home now. What have you got in Berecombe?'

'A job. Friends. A great community. A wonderful way of life.'

'What have you got in Shropshire?'

'In Ludlow? Family. I lost touch with most of my friends and teaching colleagues after the accident.'

'Seems a no-brainer to me, to borrow a phrase my Poppy uses all the time. Remember when I was at a crossroads like you? I took flight and ran home. Trouble was, when I got there, I realised everything I thought of as home was back in Devon. In Berecombe. If you're going to make dramatic decisions, it pays to know it's the right one.'

'But how can I go back to Berecombe knowing everyone will read that vile newspaper article?'

'Tush. No one will take any notice of that rubbish. Not anyone who knows you properly.'

'And I'll run the risk of bumping into Eddie.'

'Ah.'

'What do you mean, "ah"?'

'Don't you think you owe the man an explanation?'

'Possibly.'

Ruby lifted an eyebrow eloquently.

'Alright, yes, I do. Of course I do. But I don't know what to say to him.'

'What do you want to say to him?'

'I want to explain why we can't be together, and tell him that he deserves someone he can build a family with.'

'He deserves that to be said to his face, lovie.'

Ashley remained silent.

'You know what? You could have a perfectly fine life without a man, or with another man. Look at my Serena. Divorced these last fifteen years, built up a successful business.' Ruby spread her hands. 'Bought this pile of a house. All without a man. You could have that.' She wrinkled her face into well-worn grooves. 'A valid life choice. Another of my granddaughter's sayings. But I don't think you want that. I think your Eddie is like my Chet. He's the man for you.' She leaned forward. 'I lost my Chet.' Her voice faltered. 'I should have fought for him harder. Not accepted what Jimmy told me. Investigated.'

'You'd just lost your baby, Ruby. You weren't in any fit state to pursue what happened to Chet.'

'And I certainly should have given Jimmy a proper explanation as to why I couldn't marry him. Face to face an' all. I'll always regret running out on him, even if it turned out the bugger lied to me.'

'You mustn't blame yourself for that.'

'Maybe I do. Maybe I don't,' she said briskly. 'Different times and a long time ago. But *you've* got a chance to fight for your Eddie. You've got a chance to talk to him.'

'How can I, Ruby? He won't want me when he knows I can't give him what he wants.'

'That boyfriend of yours. The one you had before you went to Berecombe.'

'Piers?' Ashley was surprised at the twist in the conversation. 'I didn't know you knew about him.'

'Biddy told me. She also told me he ran out on you when you'd had your accident.' She pursed her lips. 'Not nice. Not a very honourable thing to do. Not all men are like that, Ashley.'

'I know that.'

'Eddie's not like that.'

'I know.'

'Then why not trust him a bit more? You're doing him down if you don't give him a chance to make a decision based on the truth. You're coming across as wanting to forgive him, what with all this business with Bree and Hal and whatnot, but I reckon it's the other way round. You need to ask him to forgive *you*. For not trusting him more. Maybe he's a better man than you think. Think about it, lovie. Your life in Berecombe will be good. But it'll be so much better if Eddie's a part of it. Grab any chance of happiness. I lost one chance with my Chet. I found my Alan later on and I grabbed him an' all. As hard as I could. You're a long time dead. Make the most of being alive. Besides,' she added, with a gleam in her eye, 'Eddie's my grandson. Sort of. You want to rob me of having him in me life?'

Saying she had to find some bedding to make up the sofa, she left Ashley staring vacantly into space.

Chapter Twenty-One

A fter supper, they had watched some television in a companionable silence and then Ruby had proclaimed she was tired. Ashley bundled herself up in the makeshift bed and lay staring at the shadows flickering across the ceiling, thinking over what the old woman had said. Then she drifted off to sleep, the exhausting day overtaking her.

When she woke up her decision had been made.

Ruby wouldn't let her leave without cooking her bacon and eggs, and handed her a stout package of cheese sandwiches, arguing she didn't want to have to pay the prices on the services. Ashley left just after eight, giving the woman a hard hug and promising her she'd let her know what had happened.

Once she hit the M3, she stopped and took a break. It had been easier heading out of London but maybe she was simply getting more confident. She'd decided to go and see Eddie. She needed to tell him. She needed to tell him that she loved him, that she'd always love him, but she'd set him free to have a family with someone else. She owed him that much.

But she wouldn't go straight to Exeter. There was something she needed to do first. There was a score to settle with a certain journalist. A certain journalist in Berecombe.

The offices of *The Berecombe News* were how she remembered them. On the outskirts of town housed in a dull building. She was in luck. The receptionist, recognising her from a previous visit, buzzed her straight into the news office. It was a large room, lit by harsh striplights, filled with workstations but thankfully quiet. The only other occupied desk was at the far end.

Ashley walked to where Keeley sat staring fixedly at her computer screen. She waited until the woman noticed her presence.

'Ashley!' she said in surprise, wheeling round and getting up from her desk. 'How lovely to see you. What can I do for you? Coffee?'

Ashley shook her head. 'This isn't a friendly visit.'

'Really?' Keeley's red-glossed mouth worked. She looked a little taken aback. 'I'd better sit back down then.'

'Perhaps you better had.' Ashley grabbed a chair from another workstation and sat down. She was desperate to appear confident, but her legs were shaking. 'This won't take long. I have my dog in the car and, anyway, I have somewhere far more important to be. Your article, the one about me. I wanted to let you know how hurtful I found it.'

'But it was a lovely write-up. I said lots of really positive things.'

'With lots of underlying bitching.'

'Not at all.' Keeley began to bluster just a little. 'I mentioned you organising Jimmy's funeral and being involved in the community...'

'And how I, to use your words, "popped up wherever there was a party".'

'Well, that's true. I often bump into you at social events.'

'But you insinuated I'm nothing more than a party

animal. Out for simply a good time, rather than trying to fund-raise.'

'Those things aren't mutually exclusive, Ashley.'

'You also revealed personal details about my accident.'

'Oh, come on, it was nothing that wasn't known about.'

'But only to who I choose to tell, Keeley. I don't want everyone to know what happened to me. It's none of their business. I don't want my experiences becoming town gossip.'

'Darling, this town gossips whether you like it or not.'

'True. But I prefer it if I'm the one in control of what information is in the public domain. You also implied my photographs appeared in Noah's exhibition purely because I'm his cousin.'

Keeley snorted. 'Well, that's true, isn't it?'

'He asked me because, as my cousin, he knew I take good photos. What's not true is that they would have been used in the exhibition only because of that. If they'd been awful, Noah would have found someone else.' Ashley stopped to take a breath. 'But my most serious complaint is you referencing me as some kind of siren, irresistible to men.'

'From where I was standing, that's exactly the way it looked.'

'That's how it may have appeared, but it wasn't the truth. Besides, my private life is exactly that. Private. You chose to include it in an article about community life and fund-raising where it had absolutely no relevance. Do you think about how your words impact on their subject matter? Do you think about the damage they inflict?'

'What damage?' Keeley asked scornfully but looking far less confident. 'I made you out to be glamorous and attractive, with men falling at your feet. What's damaging about that?' She huffed a little.

'And that statement shows precisely how little you know about me and the effects of your article.'

A heavy silence filled the room.

Keeley sat back on her chair, twirling a pencil through her fingers. After a long pause she said, 'Quite a list of accusations. What do you want me to do? Never mention your name again? Do you want to put in an official complaint? There's a procedure for that.'

'I'm realistic enough to know that in a small town my name is going to crop up in the local paper now and again but, from now on, kindly make it for the right reasons. And I want a printed apology.'

'I'll see what I can do.'

'I want a printed apology, otherwise I *will* make an official complaint.' Another pause. 'You're not a bad person, Keeley,' Ashley said, softening, 'but you did a bad thing making someone's personal life news fodder. It hurt me very much, so much so, I considered leaving Berecombe completely.'

Keeley had the grace to look shocked. 'Oh, don't do that, Ashley! The town would miss you. *I'd* miss you. I'd hoped we could be friends.'

Ashley stayed silent.

'Look, I'll make sure a retraction and an apology go out in the next issue.'

Ashley got up to leave.

'And I'm... I'm sorry.' Keeley cleared her throat. 'It's a tough industry, this. The paper comes down on me like a ton of bricks if the readership drops. It's the battle against everything being online, you see. Newspapers are a dying breed. Sex sells even in a seaside town full of geriatrics. I thought it might spice up the article. I didn't consider the implications. Maybe we can grab coffee and cake sometime?' she added hopefully. 'My treat. As an apology.'

'Maybe,' Ashley said and left, closing the door quietly behind her. 'But don't count on it,' she added to herself. Leaning against the wood for a second, she began to breathe normally again.

As she drove towards Exeter a light rain began to fall and she switched on the wipers. For a second, the rhythmic sound and the swish of tyres on wet tarmac caused her to flash back to that awful evening, the night of the crash. She felt her chest tighten but forced herself to breathe through it, forced herself to keep her next goal in mind. Soon, the shower stopped and blue sky broke through the clouds, so she buzzed the window down and gulped in fresh air. Tiredness must be getting to her. She'd driven so many miles in two days.

'Concentrate, woman. Get a grip!' she scolded. 'You've conquered the worst the London traffic could throw at you. Exeter will be a doddle in comparison.'

There seemed so many lanes to choose from in the approach to the city and she only had the haziest idea where Southernhay was; somewhere right in the middle, she remembered Eddie saying once, sandwiched between the hospital and the cathedral. Spotting a sign to the hospital she clung doggedly to the route, thanking the heavy city traffic for giving her time to read signs and get in the right lane.

Eventually, she turned into a road split by some green space in the middle and lined with tall red-brick terraces. She crawled along trying to spot a parking space, wondering if she'd got this right; there was an estate agent, a chiropractor, an up-market dentist. It didn't look residential. Abandoning the car on a corner, she let a relieved Bronte out of the back and hurried, on stiff uncooperative legs, to Eddie's flat. She rang the doorbell. No answer. Leaning against the front door, she was on the verge of exhausted tears. Surely she couldn't have come all this way for him not to be in? Through the fog in her brain, she heard a car door slam somewhere behind her.

'Ashley? Ash?'

Turning, she saw Eddie run over the green. He took her into his arms, and she sank into them.

'Ashley,' he breathed into her hair. 'Thank God. I just got Noah's message. I was in the car about to hot-tail it up to Ludlow to find you. Then I couldn't believe it, I saw you park up.'

They stood holding each other tightly. Then Bronte whined at their side and scrabbled at her jeans.

'She probably needs a wee,' Ashley said, vacantly. 'We've been in the car for ages.' She felt numb. Dealing with Keeley Sharma was one thing. Talking to Eddie was going to be in a different league.

Eddie fished in his pocket. 'Here, take the key. Let yourself in. I'll walk her round the block. You look all-in.' He took the dog's lead from her limp fingers and set off towards the green at speed.

Chapter Twenty-Two

A shley trudged up the stairs to Eddie's flat on the first floor. She had to hang on to the banister and haul herself up. After all the driving she was running on empty. Opening the front door, she found herself in a small hall carpeted in pale grey. Guessing, she headed left and found herself in a kitchen. It was impressive with dark granite work surfaces, shiny white cupboards and floor-to-ceiling arched windows looking out onto the street. There was a tiny table and a yellow two-seater couch, so she assumed there was no sitting room. Going back into the hall she found a bathroom and used it and then opened a door which led to a bedroom. It was unremarkable, sparsely furnished with only a few personal possessions scattered about. It also had a view over the street, so she went to see if Eddie was on his way back. Then she saw it. It was leaning against the wall, the only splash of vivid colour in an otherwise bland room. Gasping, she collapsed onto the white wicker chair.

It was her portrait. The one Jake had painted all those weeks ago in the Arts Workshop; the one he refused to sell. Looking at it afresh, she was again struck by how expertly he'd captured her inner life at that precise moment. On the brink of something, part of her glued to the past, half fearful, half hopeful, about to take a leap into a new life. She thought about how much had happened since then. The exhibition, finding out about Ruby's story, Noah and Petra getting together – sort of. Getting Enid the bicycle and the improvement in her muscle tone and health. Adopting Bronte. The astonishing revelation about Chet. And falling in love with Eddie and sharing his betrayal by Bree. But how had the painting turned up here, in Eddie's flat? She'd assumed Jake had taken it to London with him, exhibited it in a gallery somewhere, maybe even Serena's. Had Eddie bought it?

A movement in the street below caused her to look down. It was Eddie bringing Bronte back. She got up – it felt intrusive being in his bedroom – and returned to the clinical-looking kitchen.

Bronte skidded across the white tiles, leaving muddy

footprints in her wake. She landed on Ashley's lap and she held her there, anxious about what else she could ruin. The flat was most definitely not dog-friendly.

'Tea?' Eddie washed his hands in the sink and flicked the kettle on. 'This place has one of those hot-water taps but I don't trust it to boil the water hot enough.'

'Posh.'

'Yeah.' He reached down a teapot from a cupboard. 'See, you've even converted me to making it in a pot. I'm an Anglophile through and through.'

Ashley managed a laugh. 'Hate to disillusion you but I think most Brits stick a teabag in a mug now.' She caught his grimace. 'I know, it's truly shocking.' There was an awkward pause and the humour died. 'But the place doesn't seem like you somehow.' She laid her head on the sofa and watched as he toed a stool across and sat opposite her.

'You saying I'm not high class? Posh? Love that word.'

She concentrated on stroking Bronte, not able to meet his eyes. 'No.'

'You're right though, the place isn't me. The university organised it, so it wasn't my choice. I like the street, I like that it's minutes from the cathedral green, but my heart is elsewhere. I fell in love with Berecombe. And you.'

Ashley struggled up. 'About that.'

He put out a hand in defence. 'Before you say anything, I've got to apologise.'

'Whatever for?'

'I shut you out, Ash. I'm sorry.' He looked down and clasped his hands together. 'You caught me at my lowest. I'm not a man who cries much and I've never cried in front of anyone. I was...' He paused, screwing his face up. '... Embarrassed, I guess?'

'Eddie, there's absolutely nothing to feel ashamed about. God, you'd just received the worst possible news – any other reaction would have been bizarre.'

'Real men don't cry?' He attempted a smile.

'Of course real men cry. And I'd want to be with one. I was hurting so much for you and was desperate to be there for you.' She bit her lip. 'Although I have to admit I was upset you blanked me. I wanted to help but I didn't know how to.'

'I'm so sorry, Ash. Not sure anyone could have done much. I had to work my way through it, but I regret, deeply, not letting you in. I promise I'll never do that again.' He sighed. 'I know it wasn't the ideal way to bring a child into the world but, even in those circumstances, I was so proud, so happy to finally have a child.' He stopped, his lips thinning in anger. 'When I think about how she let me be in the birthing suite with her and what she went through and what I went through, I get filled with this white-hot rage. I'm not an angry person, Ash, but she's made me into one. I'm looking at people differently now, wondering what their motive is, how they could screw me over. I don't trust anyone, or not as easily. That part of me has gone.'

'That will come back. It'll take time but it'll return.'

'I know, with your help, it will.' He flashed a grin. 'Although you might have to bear with me through the rage. I might not be too easy to live with for a while.'

'You know you can trust me,' Ashley said, wondering if he could. 'And you're not designed to go through life being angry. Be angry at *her*, God knows the cow deserves it, but there are good people in the world.'

'Ones who don't lie and cheat?'

'Yes. Plenty.'

'It's not just that though.' He ran a frustrated hand through his hair, making it flop over his face. 'I feel so damned stupid. How could I have fallen for all her deceit? Why didn't I question her more? Check the condom myself?'

'Because you didn't know what she was capable of,' Ashley pointed out calmly. 'And you didn't know about Kevin then.'

'No, but I knew enough of what she was like.'

'But maybe not the lengths she'd go to. And I think she's very fond of you, maybe still in love with you.'

'How'd you figure that out?' he asked, looking startled.

'Because she wanted you to be the father of her child, even knowing you weren't,' she said softly.

He laughed bitterly. 'Spinning the positives there, Ash.'

'Maybe.'

'She's blown her chances there, good and proper. Safe to say, Bree Bauer will no longer be in my life, or my mother's. God, that's what hurt the most, you know? That she could do it to me but also take in Mom. She and Mom were such good friends.' He scrubbed a hand over his face. 'Think I was hurting about it all so much, I just wanted to be as far away from everyone as I could be. Work helped. Anonymous hotel room away from everything that was familiar. But I was wrong. I shouldn't have kept myself away from you. I promise I won't ever do that again. I know it was very wrong. We should be able to share the good times and the bad. Work through our problems together.'

Ashley wanted to reach out to him, to wrap him in her arms and rock him until his pain went away. She wanted to accept his promise that he'd be more open in the future, but knew there would be no future for them both. The kettle boiled and flicked off. The sound echoed around the sterile walls and fell into the fraught silence which lay between them. Instead of all the things she knew she ought to say, she settled for 'You bought my portrait.'

He gave a short laugh and accepted the change of subject. 'I sure did. But I acquired rather than bought it.'

'How did you persuade Jake to part with it?'

Eddie unzipped his jacket and flung it onto the sofa, where Bronte nosed it with interest. 'I got talking to Jake at the opening night of the exhibition.'

'I didn't know he was there. I didn't see him.'

Eddie shrugged. 'He was only there a second or so. Passing through on the way to Cornwall. Had a quick chat to me and Ken and left. I asked him how much he wanted for your portrait, and he looked at me kinda funny and said we could have it.' He glanced at her from under tawny lashes. 'I was going to give it to you as a wedding present.'

'A wedding present?'

'See, I want to marry you, Ashley. Nothing would make me, and I hope you, happier.'

Chapter Twenty-Three

'Oh.' 'I know it's sudden and we haven't known each other very long and there's loads of stuff to sort out but I really feel it's right. I have done for a while. Think the Bree and Hal drama clouded my thinking. I guess I thought you wouldn't be all that willing to take me on, not with all that baggage. But now, I'm as free as a bird. You and I can make our life together in any way we want, live wherever we want, however we want.' He registered her expression, slid forward on the stool and took her hands. 'What's wrong? I'll do it all again, properly, once I've bought a ring. I just wanted to get this out there between us.'

'It's not the way you've proposed.' Ashley shook her head. 'I was all ready to go back to Ludlow.'

'Yeah. Noah left me a message. I came straight here, picked up the car and was ready to head up the freeway.'

'Oh Eddie! Even risking our roads. Driving on the wrong side of the road?'

'Even that, honey.' He grinned. 'Hey, I have no idea where Ludlow is, but the SatNav would surely get me there.'

'You were chasing after me?'

'Of course I was. When I see a good thing, I'm not prepared to let it go. And I'd get to see this fabulous castle you keep going on about and Betjeman's "loveliest town" or whatever. Isn't that what he said about your hometown? About Ludlow? All good.'

'But you don't know why I was running away. You haven't asked.'

'I guessed you'd tell me. When you were ready. And jeez, guess I ran away from you, so you could say we're quits. Are you ready now? To tell me why you ran?'

'I have to be.' She slid her hands out of his and went back to hugging Bronte.

'I'm all ears. Shoot.'

'Keeley wrote an article about me in the paper.'

His brows shot up in surprise; it was obviously not what he was expecting. 'Okay,' he said, slowly.

'It wasn't very nice. Well,' Ashley corrected, 'on the surface it's perfectly nice, complimentary even.'

'But?'

'But anyone with half a brain will now see me as a publicity-seeking man magnet. But it's worse than that. It made me feel exposed. I'm not like Petra, or Noah even; I hate the spotlight being on me. I don't have the confidence for it, not since the accident – maybe I never did. I thought I'd done some good things since arriving in Berecombe. Organising Jimmy's funeral, taping Ruby's history, being part of a community in a way I haven't felt for ages. That bitchy piece of chip-wrap cheapened everything I've achieved.'

'Chip-wrap?'

'They used to wrap fish and chips in old newspapers before Health and Safety banned it,' she explained.

'Euuuw. I should think so too.' Eddie pulled a disgusted face. 'But there's your answer. One day it's headline news, the next it's paper round a take-out.'

'There is a saying that goes something like that,' she admitted. 'It's just as well you hadn't hit the road. I ended up not going back to Ludlow. I went to see Ruby instead.'

'In London?'

Ashley nodded.

'Jeez, kiddo. No wonder you're beat.'

'We had a good talk. She made me see the sense in a lot of things.'

'Wise woman, my adopted grandma.'

'She gave me the courage to go and confront Keeley about what she'd written.'

'Wow! How did that go?'

'She apologised. Sort of.' Ashley shrugged. 'Think that was the most I was going to get out of her, but she's also promised to print an apology.'

'Great result. It must have taken a lot of courage to confront her. I'm proud of you.'

'I still have to face the good residents of Berecombe though.'

He took her hand again. 'The people who know you will know you for the good, kind, thoughtful person you are. The committed teacher, the person who is generous with her time when giving to the community, to make it a better place.'

'Ruby said much the same.'

He shrugged. 'There you go. Like I said, wise woman. You can't control what strangers think of you and I don't think you should care. The ones who matter are the ones you care about. Noah knows you're not like that, Biddy and Petra do too.' He raised her hand to his mouth and kissed it gently. 'And so do I.' He stared at her intently. 'But that can't have been all that made you want to get out of town?'

She shook her head, willing the tears away. 'It

wasn't.' She sucked in an enormous breath. 'I had some bad news. News I was expecting, I suppose, but that I've been pretending wouldn't come. Ignoring the fact that it would come.'

'And that is?'

'I had a letter from my consultant.' She paused, her eyes brilliant with unshed tears. 'It confirmed it.' She took in another deep breath and rushed the rest out. 'I can't have children, Eddie. I definitely can't have your children, or anybody's. I can't give you the family you so desperately want.'

He blinked. 'But we knew this was a possibility.'

She nodded and said on a sob, 'But that was before, when we thought you had Hal. I always consoled myself with the idea that, if I couldn't give you a child, you'd... we'd have Hal. And now' – tears ran down her face unchecked – 'now I know for definite that it can't be me who has your children, I have to give you up to someone who can. I can't let you go through your life not having the one thing you most want. Oh, Eddie, that's why I can't marry you. Not now. Not ever.' She struggled blindly to her feet, gathered Bronte's lead and stumbled into the hall.

Chapter Twenty-Four

Eddie got to the door first. He put his back to it and faced her. 'No,' he said calmly.

'What?'

'I said no.'

'Eddie, get out of my way. I'm tired and I just want to go home.'

He crossed his arms. 'No.'

Ashley sagged. She was exhausted and not in the mood for him to suddenly turn Neanderthal. It was very unlike the Eddie she knew. 'I don't know what you want.'

'I want you. I want us. I want us to go back into that room and talk this through. After all we've both been through these past few months and especially the last few days, that's the least we can do. We can work this out.'

'There's nothing more to say.'

One brow quirked. 'You think so? I don't agree. You think so little of me that you think I would rather go have a baby with some random woman just to achieve my aim of having a family?'

'Don't be crude, Eddie, it's not like you.'

'I will if it forces some sense into you. Go back into the kitchen, sit down on the sofa, I'll make the tea and we'll talk. Or you can sleep first, then we'll talk. But hear me now, I'm not giving up on us. Even if we're not married yet, I still want you through sickness and health, through the good times and the bad, kids or no kids. All we need is each other.'

She stared at him unblinking. It was so unlike the Eddie she knew to come over masterful and alpha male that she didn't know whether to be infuriated or turned on. Turning on her heel, she retraced her steps and flung herself, a little sulkily, onto the sofa. She watched as he re-boiled the kettle and made tea.

When he handed her the mug, she clutched it to her, needing its heat.

He sat opposite her, on the stool again, but remained silent. Then he jumped up and produced a packet of biscuits. Handing them over, he said, 'Maybe you need some sugar. Eat a cookie.'

'Biscuit.'

'And she's back.'

'Don't laugh at me.'

'Wouldn't dare.' He waited while she ate three biscuits and drank the tea. 'So, what's all this about, Ash?'

'I've told you. I can't have children, so I think it's better if we stop seeing each other.'

'That's all very good and noble of you to give me up and all, but what if I don't want to give you up?'

'Eddie, you've always made it abundantly clear, from practically the first time we met, how keen you were on having a family. I can't give you that so it's best if we finish and you have children with someone else.'

Eddie tutted. 'Noah warned me you don't do compromise.'

'Well, Noah won't mind if I kill him quietly in his sleep then, will he? How dare you two discuss me!'

He gave a short laugh. 'We didn't. He mentioned once that you weren't good on compromise when faced with a dilemma.'

'Did he?' Ashley was still furious.

'Was that what was behind the impulse trip to London?'

Ashley couldn't meet his eyes. The anger fled; she was too tired to be indignant. She stroked the plush fabric of the sofa instead. 'I wasn't sure what I was doing. I didn't know where I needed to be. I couldn't face my parents and going back to Ludlow seemed too much like admitting failure. I couldn't face returning to Berecombe either. I thought Ruby might help. She told me, in no uncertain terms, that I owed you an explanation about why I was ending our relationship. That I needed to tell you face to face. She also said I was underestimating you. Big time. That I ought to trust you more.'

'Good advice. Thank you, Ruby.'

Ashley looked at him then. 'I don't appreciate your sarcasm.'

'Hey, I'm not being sarcastic here. I think it's a major step to come back and face the consequences of your decision.' He shrugged. 'Except I'm not accepting it.'

'Eddie, we've been through all this.' She sighed wearily.

'And I said to you once before: I'd rather be with you and risk not having children than be with anyone else.'

'Which is great until we argue and you throw my inability to have children back at me.'

'Which I might do in the heat of the moment, in which case we'd fight and make up, but I really doubt I'd ever be that cruel.'

'No, I don't think you would be.'

'So, what's the problem – what's the *real* problem – here?'

'I'm a failure,' she burst out. 'I'm an absolute total failure. I can't do the one thing my body is uniquely designed to do.' She waved her arms around wildly, making Bronte growl. 'Everywhere I go I hear of teenage girls getting pregnant when they don't want to be, of women trying and falling pregnant instantly. I read articles about celebs who are forty-seven and manage to have a baby. Even in Berecombe there's Millie with Bobbie, and Mike from the theatre with his Hollywood star wife Dora with their toddler Lily, and probably working on another. At this rate they're going to have to expand the school with the baby boom that's going on. And I can't do it. *I* can't have a baby!'

'You got this letter from your consultant?' He took the mug out of her flailing hands.

She scrabbled through her bag, found a tissue, paused to wipe her face and blow her nose and then found the letter. 'It's here. Why do you want to read it?'

'For better or worse, remember? We face things together.' He took it off her and scanned the contents, frowning. Then he shook his head. 'It's one man's opinion, Ash. In his opinion he thinks you shouldn't bear children. *In his opinion.*'

'He's a medical professional, Eddie,' she said bitterly. 'A specialist in his field. He should know what he's on about.'

He shrugged. 'Maybe. But he's one man. One medical professional amongst many. He's a what? Bone guy? Orthopaedist? We can find another specialist, an obstetrician, seek another opinion, see where that leads us. Go private if we have to.'

'But that costs money.'

He grinned. 'Hey, babe, I've got money. I'm being paid far more for the TV work than I ever was at the university.'

'I can't take your money,' she said, appalled.

'Think that's the "for better" bit. We're a partnership; we share. In fact, I'd be offended if any wife of mine wouldn't take my money.'

'All this talk of money. You're so American sometimes.'

'Sure am. And you're so English. Didn't you know you can solve most problems if you throw enough money at them?'

She let a giggle escape. He was being so preposterous. So determined.

'Okay, maybe that's not strictly true but it can sure help sometimes.' He slid to kneel on the floor and took her hands again. 'Maybe you can't have a kid, maybe you can. Maybe we adopt or use a surrogate. Or just decide to get another damned dog. If we want a family, there are ways. Hell, we're a family now. I want to be with you, whether that means it's us two and Bronte, or a load of kids running riot round the homestead.'

'Ruby said I ought to ask you to forgive me,' Ashley said breathlessly, the emotion choking her. She felt the tiniest spark of hope. Could it be possible everything would be alright?

'What for?'

'For not trusting you enough to make your decision knowing the truth. The truth about me.'

'Nothing to forgive, Ashley.' He kissed her hands again, his breath warm on her fingers. 'Nothing at all. I love you and all that brings – baby or no baby, health or no health. I want to be with you and look after you, laugh with you, grow old with you. I love you, Ashley. My heart's fit to bursting with all the love I have for you. And if I don't give it to you, then just what do you suggest I do with it? And you may have noticed I'm on my knees here, so what do you say? Will you marry me? For whatever comes our way, through hard times and good, through thick and thin, through clouds and sunshine. Will you be my soulmate, my life partner?'

'Oh, Eddie,' she cried, bursting into tears. 'Whatever did I do to deserve you?'

'Guess that's a yes?'

'Do you know what you're taking on with me?'

'Hell, baby, do you know what you're taking on with me?'

'I do. I know you're the kindest, most thoughtful man I'll ever hope to meet.'

'And?' he asked, the confident façade slipping just a little.

'It's a yes.' She flung her arms around his neck. 'I love you too, so much, and it's a yes. Yes, I'll marry you. Through the good times and the bad, through sickness and health, through the laughter and the tears. I'll marry you!'

Epilogue

Two years later

Biddy had gone overboard with the bunting again. Blue and pink triangles flapped in the October breeze; she'd hedged her bets. And, practical as ever, she thought the new managers of Millie Vanilla's could use it in the café after the party. It was one of those gifts of a day when autumn gives up the fight temporarily and lets summer have a final hurrah. The sea danced sparkles in the sunshine, and there was just enough wind to whip up white horses on the waves, and rosy cheeks on the children running around the terrace. After the horrors of the past year, it was good to have things opening up again and adjust to the "new normal".

Millie rescued Bobbie the Baby, now a sturdy

toddler, from chasing seagulls, gathered her onto her lap and collapsed thankfully onto the chair next to Eddie. 'So, you decided on a girl's name eventually then?'

'Hey there, Bobbie.' He pulled a face, making her giggle. Addressing Millie, he added, 'Sofia Ann McQueen. Named after the two grandmas.'

'How pretty.' She grinned. 'And how tactful. Are your parents going to get over?'

'When it's possible. When they're able to travel we've said they can stay as long as they want. Guess when I decided to settle in another country, I didn't figure in how difficult it would be to travel to see them as often as I'd like.'

'It must have been so hard,' Millie sympathised. 'It's been awful how the crisis has kept families apart. Shame they've missed so much and now they've missed the naming party.'

Eddie nodded to where a live cam had been set up. 'Alex and Eleri are live-streaming it for us, so they don't miss out too much. Not the same as being here but at least they can see what's going on.'

'That's a great idea. We must make sure we give them a big Berecombe wave later. And I'm sorry we couldn't all celebrate your wedding.'

'Yeah, though we were lucky to even get married and,

to be honest, a quick trip to the Registrar's Office suited us both fine.'

Millie chuckled. 'That's what Ashley *told* you. Are you sure she didn't mind missing out on all the big white frock and fuss?'

'Point taken. Maybe we can have a party when all this has blown over? Maybe when my parents can make it?'

'You're on and, let's face it, Berecombe doesn't need much of an excuse to hold a party. The town even finds a way in the middle of a pandemic – and isn't it good to get out and meet people in real life again? I've become all Zoomed-out, although it was a blessing in lockdown. Hope the weather holds, it's glorious today.' She lifted her face to the sunshine.

'Can't argue with you there.' He took in a great breath of salty air. 'So glad Ash and I decided to make Berecombe our home. It's a good place to raise kids.'

'And Berecombe's very glad to have you. We wouldn't be without our amazing art teacher and fund-raiser, and TV personality, for anything. It's certainly been busy this summer. I've never known the town so crowded. I suppose it's because people couldn't go abroad. An ill wind and all that. Hopefully, they'll remember what a fabulous place the Devon seaside is and return next year. The summer saved the café.' She shuddered slightly. 'It was all so uncertain early this year.

Speaking of work, will you be able to resume filming your TV programme again soon? I loved the first series you did.'

'Hope so.'

She smiled at him. 'How are you settling into the new house? It was Biddy's old one, wasn't it, before she moved into the bungalow with Arthur? It's the most gorgeous place, really convenient for town, and the views are to die for.'

'It's perfect. So good to have the extra space, especially as we were stuck inside so much. And it meant we could have Ash's parents to stay.'

'Always good to have help with new babies. I only had this wriggler.' At this Bobbie slid from her mother's lap and wobbled off in the direction of Jed. 'One baby was quite enough for me.'

'Speaking of babies, here she is now.' He stood up as Ashley appeared, carrying their daughter. 'All fed and changed?' he asked, kissing his wife. 'I could have done it, you know.'

Ashley grinned, joy radiating out of her. 'You wouldn't have got anywhere near! I had an army of volunteers, including Noah – I think he's gone all broody. All done now though, your turn next time.'

'Gotta love me a poopy diaper.'

'Then they're all yours, husband of mine. I won't

complain. Do I sit here?' She settled on a bench, which was covered in plump pink and white cushions, set against the sun-warmed wall. 'Mum's just behind me.'

Ann handed the other baby over. 'Here you go, Eddie, all sleepy and sweet-smelling. For the moment, anyway.'

Eddie sat next to Ashley, holding his second child. He kissed his wife's cheek. 'Have I told you how much I love you?'

'Not today!'

'Very remiss of me. I love you, Ashley.'

Ashley watched the deep groove appear at the side of his mouth as he smiled. She loved that dimple. With difficulty, as her arms were full of baby, she reached up and kissed it. 'And I love you, Eddie McQueen. With all my heart.'

'Are we finally all ready now?' Biddy asked. She peered over her glasses. 'At last? If we could all settle down. Noah, could you please sit down?'

Noah grinned apologetically and sat down next to Petra, slinging an arm around her shoulders and kissing her enthusiastically. With the crisis, she'd been spending all her time in Berecombe and they'd finally committed to being a couple. Wearing a red '50s dress which clung to her curves in outrageous fashion, she'd kicked off proceedings by leading the re-formed community choir in an impromptu rendition of Stevie Wonder's 'Isn't She

Lovely', which had made everyone cry. Beryl, incongruous in virginal white, husband Arthur and granddaughter Zoe sat at a nearby table, with Zoe cheerfully minding the dogs in the resurrected doggie creche. The Tizzards occupied a couple of tables put together to accommodate their large and noisy clan. Amy from the bookshop sat hand-in-hand with her handsome writer boyfriend Patrick. Tash, immaculate in a turquoise skirt suit, perched on fiancé Kit's knee. Dora and Mike, with their little girl squirming on her father's lap, sat at another table, with eyes only for each other and Mike's hand tenderly resting on his wife's stomach; in the new year their little family would grow. Millie and Jed joined Ann and Richard Lydden, along with Davina and Pete, and were already getting stuck into the champagne, with Jed trying to keep his glass away from his mischievous daughter. And Ruby, wearing a pale-pink twinset and pearls, sat with her daughter Serena at a table for two, both demurely sipping tea.

My friends and most of my family are here, Ashley thought happily, settling back against the sun-drenched wall, her baby daughter asleep and content in her arms. Tears prickled. Happy tears, thankful and possibly hormonal ones. She had so much to be appreciative of and whispered a prayer of gratitude. They'd all come through impossibly grim times and were safe. She had her darling husband and, despite all the odds, twin babies. Her family was complete. And while she couldn't recommend months of bed rest and a planned c-section at seven months undertaken during a pandemic, it had all been worth it. She looked around, caught Ruby's eye and smiled. The old woman had come through, too. For Ruby, Covid had been one more challenge in a long eventful life.

The old woman raised her teacup in salute. 'Thank you,' she mouthed, dabbing a snowy white handkerchief to teary eyes and then pressing her hand to her breast. 'Thank you so much.'

Ashley mouthed back, 'You're welcome.' Naming the babies had been an almost impossible task but she knew the final decision had meant a huge amount to Ruby; it meant a lot – to all of them.

Biddy harrumphed and tapped a pen against her glass to get everyone's attention. The guests sat up to attention, nudged one another and shifted towards her in order to listen. Those who knew the woman well exchanged grins.

'We are gathered here today,' she began, a little portentously, 'as a celebration and a welcome to two new residents of our happy little town.' She stopped, seeming to choke up and then continued. 'In this last year community has never been more important. Not just in

Devon but across the world. Our way of life and the freedoms we took for granted have been threatened. In some cases, lives have gone and we've sadly lost members of our close-knit community, which has hit us hard.' Tears sparkled in Biddy's eyes. She sucked in a breath and continued. 'But Berecombe rallied, as only Berecombe can. Folk shopped local where they could. The Smalls set up their wonderful delivery service from their farm shop and kept us all going with milk, butter and cream, not to mention delicious bacon. Tessa Tizzard baked up a storm and she and Ken drove around town providing us with home-baked bread. The WI community volunteers got prescriptions to those shielding or ill and this very café cooked utterly delicious hot food for delivery or takeaway. We faced the crisis head-on in our usual way; with humour, fortitude and resilience.' One or two in the audience sniffed and dabbed at their eyes, moved by what she'd said. Then she coughed and added, with mock humility, 'You'll be glad to know *I* used my lockdown to write another three novels.'

Someone groaned.

'That'll be enough cheek from you, young Louis Tizzard,' she snapped, and everyone laughed.

'But now we come to the main reason we're here. Our town, our lovely close-knit, wonderful town has two new members. In this age of uncertainty one thing brings joy and hope and we're surely in need of both. A new baby brings all that is shiny, bright and innocent. Hope for the future, joy for us all.' At this more sniffles could be heard. 'With our newest residents, just arrived, we have a double, miraculous gift of optimism. For we have not one new baby but two. We wish them a world full of peace, tolerance and happiness, and most of all health. May they be rich in friends and family and let love surround and protect them always. Welcome to Berecombe and the world, and may blessings rain upon you both. Welcome, Sofia Ann McQueen and Chet James McQueen.'

Acknowledgments

I needed a lot of help to write this one! I hope I've included everyone this time.

My sincere thanks go to the very lovely and talented Colin Simmonds who furnished me with details of a painter's life, and to Dr Pinky Jain and Dr Linzi McKerr of Worcester University for information on academia. My grateful thanks go to Julia Roebuck who opened up the world of Morris Dancing, Wendy Jones who, as always, gave medical information, and Leah Larson and Greg Poulos for help on all things USA. Janice Rosser and the Helen Vereker Singers helped with what it means to be in a community choir and Janice Preston provided information about art classes. Thank you all! I'm also grateful that writing this book meant I had an excuse to discuss my mother's childhood wartime memories with her. She also helped with the titles. Thanks mum! I'm so grateful these people gave up their precious time to share their expertise; any mistakes are very much all mine.

Charlotte Ledger and her team at One More Chapter helped shape this book with brilliant editing and I am eternally grateful for their enthusiasm and expertise.

And finally, a huge thank you to you, the reader, for buying, borrowing, reading, reviewing, and supporting my books. If one thing the past two years have proved, it's that reading and books are more important than ever.

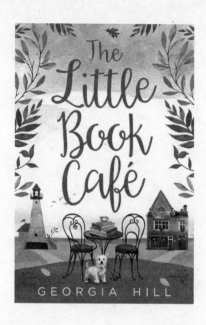

You will also love *The Little Book Café*, another charming and heartwarming series from Georgia Hill...

Tash, Emma and Amy couldn't be more different. A successful estate agent who has her life pretty much on track, Tash has ticked all the boxes. Hasn't she? Emma is a budding writer who yearns to flex her writing skills and shake up her life... And then there's Amy, the manager of The Little Book Café, a hopeless romantic who had her heart broken but refuses to give up on love.

Brought together by good books and delicious cake, they are in for a year like no other...

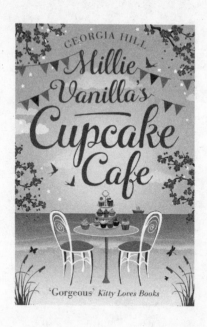

Don't miss Millie Vanilla's Cupcake Café!

Millie Vanilla's Cupcake Café is struggling as a multi-national chain of cafés moves in on its territory. Despite baking up a storm in a bid to save it, Millie's distracted by falling head over heels for the very gorgeous and mysterious Jed.

But when she discovers Jed's been keeping secrets, she faces a new dilemma – is it finally time to hang up her apron and start an exciting life somewhere new? Or is everything she's ever wanted right under her nose, just waiting for her to reach out and take it?

Be sure to treat yourself to a copy of *While I Was Waiting*...

Tired of her life in London, freelance illustrator Rachel buys the beautiful but dilapidated Clematis Cottage and sets about creating the home of her dreams.

But tucked away behind the water tank in the attic and left to gather dust for decades is an old biscuit tin containing letters, postcards and a diary telling the story of Henrietta Trenchard-Lewis, the love she lost in the Great War and the girl who was left behind...

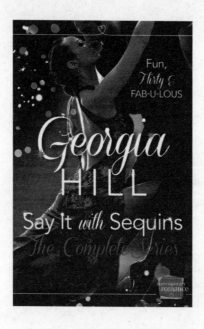

And check out *Say It with Sequins*, the fun, flirty and FAB-U-LOUS romantic comedy series perfect for lovers of *Strictly Come Dancing*!

Who Dares Dances is a reality TV show with a difference. Not only do contestants have to learn to dance, they also face a series of bizarre challenges. But these challenges are nothing compared to the scandals happening on – and off – the ballroom floor!

As the celebrities get closer to both the winners' trophy and their professional partners it's all to dance for…

YOUR NUMBER ONE STOP

ONE MORE CHAPTER

FOR PAGETURNING BOOKS

One More Chapter is an
award-winning global
division of HarperCollins.

Sign up to our newsletter to get our
latest eBook deals and stay up to date
with our weekly Book Club!
<u>Subscribe here.</u>

Meet the team at
<u>www.onemorechapter.com</u>

Follow us!
🐦 <u>@OneMoreChapter_</u>
f <u>@OneMoreChapter</u>
📷 <u>@onemorechapterhc</u>

Do you write unputdownable fiction?
We love to hear from new voices.
Find out how to submit your novel at
<u>www.onemorechapter.com/submissions</u>